BIBLE KidVENTURES

STORIES OF DANGER AND COURAGE

Deadly Exhibition

Trapped!

Attack!

Escape!

Jeanne Gowen Dennis and Sheila Seifert

Tyndale House Publishers, Inc.
Carol Stream, Illinois

Bible KidVentures: Stories of Danger and Courage

© 2016 Jeanne Gowen Dennis and Sheila Seifert

A Focus on the Family book published by Tyndale House Publishers, Inc., Carol Stream, Illinois 60188

Focus on the Family and the accompanying logo and designs are federally registered trademarks of Focus on the Family, 8605 Explorer Drive, Colorado Springs, CO 80920.

TYNDALE and Tyndale's quill logo are registered trademarks of Tyndale House Publishers, Inc.

Cover design by Beth Sparkman

Cover illustration copyright © Rick Fairlamb/Astound. All rights reserved.

Interior illustrations by Ron Adair

These books were originally published in 2003 as separate books:
Deadly Exhibition (ISBN 978-0-7814-3897-1), *Trapped!* (ISBN 978-0-7814-3898-8), *Attack!* (ISBN 978-0-7814-3894-0), and *Escape!* (ISBN 978-0-7814-3895-7).

For manufacturing information regarding this product, please call 1-800-323-9400.

Library of Congress Cataloging-in-Publication Data for this title can be found at www.loc.gov.

ISBN 978-1-58997-865-2

Printed in the United States of America

22   21   20   19   18   17   16
7   6   5   4   3   2   1

To my wonderful grandchildren, Emma, Noah, and Lucy.
I'm so grateful to God for you.

JEANNE DENNIS

To Glen, Jeshua, Nick, and Austin—
Thanks for the adventure of family; I'm privileged to be a part of yours.

SHEILA SEIFERT

CONTENTS

THE ADVENTURE BEGINS

Have you ever wanted to witness the Red Sea opening or the walls of Jericho falling? This collection of stories takes you into the middle of the action of exciting Bible events.

In each story, you are the main character. What happens is up to you! Through your choices, you can receive great rewards, get into big trouble, or even lose your life.

Your goal is to choose well and survive.

Start at the beginning of each story. Each time you are faced with a choice, make a decision. Then follow the instructions, and turn to the correct page to see what happens next. You'll be flipping pages, but that's part of the fun!

When you're done with one story, you can always start over again at the beginning. There are lots of possibilities packed into each adventure and many different endings.

Remember, you make the decisions. See if you can survive the dangers, and have courage no matter what happens!

Your adventure begins now.

Deadly
Expedition

Deadly Expedition

"The Egyptians are coming! Help us! Moses, help us!"

Everyone around you is screaming. You stand up on a cart to see over the heads of thousands of people around you—about six hundred thousand men and lots more women and children. In the distance you see a cloud of dust. Could it be Pharaoh's army? Only a couple of days ago, Pharaoh let you and all the other Israelite slaves go free. Why would he have changed his mind?

Your younger sisters, Mary and Mariah, are screaming. They are identical twins with identical high-pitched shrills. They sound a lot younger than their ten years.

"That's enough," your father says.

They cover their mouths with their hands, but their eyes remain large. You know that their hearts are probably beating as rapidly as yours. You strain your eyes to see in the distance as your mother tries to quiet your baby brother, Kilion. He is screaming, not from fear, but because he loves to yell.

You look back at the cloud of dust on the distant horizon, then in the opposite direction at the Red Sea. Your hands feel clammy. There is nowhere to go! Your escape route is blocked by water!

"Now what?" you ask.

"Moses must have a plan," your mother says. "He wouldn't bring us here to die." You hear uncertainty in her voice. She hands you a crust of bread, the last of the bread that she baked at your home in Egypt. It is stale, almost without taste, but you gnaw on it as the others in your family struggle to eat their pieces of bread.

A man shouts to Moses, "Why did you bring us all the way into the desert to die? Didn't Egypt have enough graves?"

A woman adds, "It would have been better to remain slaves in Egypt than to die out here."

Mary and Mariah begin to scream again in their high-pitched voices, "We're going to die! We're going to die!"

CHOICE ONE: If you agree with your sisters and begin yelling, turn to page 83.

CHOICE TWO: If you tell your sisters to be quiet so you can hear what Moses is saying, turn to page 5.

Your father leans forward toward a friend. "Can you tell what Moses is saying?"

"I sent Esau to the front," the friend says. "He'll tell us."

You watch Moses until he has finished talking. Then you spot Esau in the crowd, weaving his way back to his family at a run. He has been your best friend since you were little.

When he gets close, his father yells, "Well? What did he say? How are we supposed to escape?"

Esau holds up a hand and tries to catch his breath. The cloud of dust behind you from the approaching chariots is enormous, darkening the entire horizon.

"He told us to stand firm and watch to see how God delivers us," Esau answers. "He said that the Lord would fight for us, and we need only to be still."

Your mother shakes her head. "Then that's that." She does not stop Kilion from yelling. Your father looks away. Mary and Mariah scream.

Esau's father scoffs. "I've seen how God provides." He points to the welts on his back. "I've seen it my whole life."

You have welts, too, from being beaten. Your muscles still ache from bending over to make Egyptian bricks these last several years. Why did you believe Moses? When he talked about taking everyone to the Promised Land, you had such high hopes. You dreamed of being free and having plenty to eat. You wonder how you ever thought you could get to the "land flowing with milk and honey."

"Is all hope lost?" you ask to no one in particular as you step down from the cart.

Your father puts his arm around your shoulders and says, "I don't know. God did send plagues of frogs, locusts, and blood-filled water to our enemies."

Your mother adds, "And He punished the Egyptians by killing their firstborn sons." They look at each other as if trying to believe. You turn away from your family and look at the pillar-like cloud that shows God is with you. The screams around you are increasing. Pharaoh's army is drawing nearer.

CHOICE ONE: If you wait to see how God provides,
go to page 7.

CHOICE TWO: If you take matters in your own hands,
go to page 10.

"I think we should listen to Moses," you tell your mother and give her what you hope is an encouraging smile. "It's going to be okay." Your mother nods but then bites her top lip and looks down.

"Rhoda, we'll be fine," your father repeats. Your parents' eyes meet. You turn away from them and hear a sound as if a strong wind is blowing. Your eyes settle on the pillar of cloud again. Is it moving?

"Look!" you say, pointing to it. "The pillar of cloud!" That cloud has led you every day and then turned into a pillar of fire at night to guide you. Moses says that the pillar is God leading His people, and that you are one of His people. Every time the cloud has moved, you have moved. Every time it has stopped, you have camped and eaten gritty food—food coated with desert sand. Again, you are amazed at the cloud's enormous size. It looks like a desert windstorm piled up in a column.

"The cloud!" another voice yells. Soon everyone is watching God's pillar. Slowly it moves around the entire Israelite camp. You can smell the muddy water near the shore of the Red Sea. When the cloud reaches the desert sand behind you, it spreads out like a wall.

"The Egyptians will never be able to get through that," Esau says. You agree. With the pillar of cloud between you and the Egyptians, you cannot even see the dust cloud that the Egyptians were making. You are glad. If you cannot see them, then they cannot see you.

A cheer goes up from the crowd.

Esau laughs. "That was cool."

Esau's father sneers. "Moses will probably say that the cloud is God protecting us. He tries to use everything to his advantage."

"You don't think God is protecting us?" you ask. Esau's father rolls his eyes.

Esau says, "Let's not worry about who did what. The cloud is between us and the Egyptians. That will give us some time to figure out what to do next."

The night grows dark behind the cloud, but on your side, the pillar of fire lights the whole camp. You do not like sitting still.

CHOICE ONE: If you continue waiting to see what God will do, go to page 68.

CHOICE TWO: If you begin figuring out what your family needs to do next, go to page 39.

◆   ◆   ◆

Why would Moses lead all of these people into a trap? With the cold Red Sea on one side and Pharaoh's ferocious army bearing down on you from the other, there is nowhere to go.

"Moses must have been crazy to lead us here," you mutter to Esau. "He's not a skilled leader like the Egyptians were. We shouldn't have trusted him."

Esau nods. "Yeah, my dad is pretty upset about it, but what can we do?"

"I don't know, but I'll think of something."

Your parents are busy taking care of the younger kids. You cannot bear to see the worry in their faces. You are the eldest. You must figure out how to keep your family together and alive. The dust cloud in the distance is getting larger, which means that Pharaoh's army is getting closer. You can smell the dust in the air.

You slowly move away from your tent so that your family will not notice that you are leaving. You can think of only two possible ways to fix the situation.

CHOICE ONE: If you try to find an escape route for
your family, go to page 11.

CHOICE TWO: If you throw yourself on the mercy of
Pharaoh, go to page 81.

You spit into the sand at your feet. The time to trust others—
Moses, Pharaoh, and God—is gone. You take off running along
the edge of the Red Sea. You are going to find a shallow place where
you and your family can cross, even if it takes you all night.

After running for some time, you shout to the sea, "Tell me your
secrets!" The water remains calm except for an occasional plop from
an insect or rodent.

The sky darkens, but the pillar of fire in the distance gives you
just enough light to see. You continue along the shoreline of the Red
Sea. No matter how far you go, it is much too wide and deep for
your family to cross safely because no one in your family knows how
to swim. Besides, the wind has picked up, and waves have started
forming.

You stop and try to catch your breath. Your mouth is dry, but the
seawater smells like dead fish. You look into the darkness ahead of
you and then back to the distant pillar of fire behind you.

CHOICE ONE: If you turn back and start looking
for a place to cross in the opposite direction,
go to page 42.

CHOICE TWO: If you keep going in the same direction
until you find an escape route, go to page 32.

◆ ◆ ◆

"Help!" you scream. You stand up, trip on a stone, and fall, hitting your chin on a jagged rock. Ignoring the pain, you scramble to get up. The sand slides beneath you, and you taste its dirty flavor once again. "Help!"

It is too late. The man is right behind you. You cannot escape him now. You shut your eyes to prepare for death, but suddenly the man groans. Thump. It sounds like someone fell to the ground. Cautiously, you look behind you. An Israelite is standing over the enemy's body. He has saved you!

"Thank you!" you say. You want to cry, you are so happy.

"Run home," the Israelite says sternly. "This is no place for children."

You nod. There is nothing you want more than to run home. You slip around the body and try to run away, but you are too sore. You limp toward camp. The scrape on your chin throbs with pain. Yet, all the way home, you take deep breaths of warm air and relish the smells of the desert plants. You feel grateful to be alive. You had no idea that battles were so dangerous.

When your father comes home that night, you volunteer to clean his sword. It is really heavy. You look the other way as you wipe the blood from it. The smell reminds you of the dead enemy soldier. You wrinkle your nose.

Afterward you hold the sword just as the Israelite soldier did who saved your life. You try to use it, but it is too heavy. You want to be able to defend yourself if another enemy attacks. You pick it up again.

"No. No," says your father, laughing. "Hold it this way." He shows you. You mimic his hold. "That's better," he says. He shows you how to use it. From now on, you plan to practice every day. You do not know what lies ahead, but you want to be prepared.

THE END

◆ ◆ ◆

You hate the sun. You hate the sand. You are tired of noise, and sick to death of eating manna at every meal. You see no reason why you should obey your parents and not be with your friends, but you decide to obey anyway.

After a few days of obeying, you find it easier to be grateful for what you have. Soon you choose not to complain, no matter how you feel. When your friends bug you, you try to remember what it felt like when you were on the other side of the Red Sea, away from them and God's pillar of protection. When you have to carry water and it sloshes onto your clothes, or you collect manna when it is not supposed to be your turn, you try to remember how much harder it was making bricks as a slave. Besides, water sliding down your throat is a great feeling in a desert; and manna has a honey-sweet smell that is almost like perfume.

"Why are you such a goody-two-sandals?" Esau asks you one day.

You shrug and shake your head. "I get as discouraged as you do, but I also know that without God, life is a lot worse."

Esau looks at you strangely, but he starts hanging around you more than he used to. As long as he does not complain, you let him.

You can ignore the complaints outside your tent, but it is harder to ignore the ones inside. Almost every day, Mary says, "Do we have to eat manna again?"

"It's a wonderful gift from God," you say. "You know, when I was—"

"Oh please," says Mariah holding up her hands. "Not that story about almost starving to death. I don't have to be grateful about eating the same thing every day just because you were hungry once."

Mary makes a disgusted sound. "Come along, Mariah. Let's go find Leah."

The next morning, you are determined to keep quiet as you gather manna with your sisters. You look up at the sky.

You say, "Isn't it great how God sends us manna to eat every morning?"

Mariah yells, "Mother! I'm getting another lecture on being grateful for what I have." As the twins hurry away from you, you shake your head. Your mother comes up behind you and rubs your back.

"Everyone's complaining nowadays," she says.

"But we have it so easy," you say. "God has really blessed us. We're free, we have food and water, and God loves us."

Then one day, your father comes to you. "Let's talk about everything God has done for us. I'm tired and discouraged. I just need to hear it one more time."

From then on, you do not care what people say. You tell everyone who will listen about how wonderful God is.

THE END

◆ ◆ ◆

"I would like to travel with you for a while," you say. "And I want to work to pay for my food and my place in this caravan. But if we ever travel to the other side of the sea, I must try to find my family."

"Of course," Haran says.

"And perhaps you could even help me find out where my people might have gone." You give Haran a hopeful smile.

Haran throws back his head and laughs. "And what brings more pleasure in life than going out of one's way for a stranger? We will help you find your people, Little Pilgrim."

"Thank you," you say. You travel with them for many days across the hot desert and realize that Haran is going quite a bit out of his way to help you. He sends out scouts to try to find news of Israel's people. You are amazed at the man's generosity. In some ways, you almost hope that you will not have to leave Haran's caravan.

You have grown used to eating horsemeat and drinking tea. Many camels are laden with sacks full of goods. The sacks still smell like the spices that Haran traded for the goods. Even the barking of the caravan's dogs and the strange words of the traders are beginning to sound familiar, although you do not yet understand their language. In spite of all of this, there is an ache in your heart that will continue until you find your family.

Then one day, Haran calls you to him, "Little Pilgrim," he says, "we have found your people." He points to a dot in the distance. "They are there at a mountain called Sinai."

"You are certain it is the Israelites?" you ask.

Haran nods and then looks at you closely. "Are you certain that you wish to leave us?"

You shake your head. "I do not wish to leave you, but my place is with my people."

"A good answer," Haran says. "May the gods be with you, Little Pilgrim."

"May the God of Moses bless you for your kindness to me," you answer. Haran nods his head once to receive your blessing. Then he gives you food and water for a day's journey.

As you leave the caravan, a lump catches in your throat. Just then Haran yells, "If you change your mind, Little Pilgrim, you can find us to the east."

"And if you wish to join my people," you call back, "you will always be welcome at my family's table."

Your heart is lighter as you continue on your way. You reach the camp in the late afternoon but are surprised at what you see. A smoky cloud hangs over the mountain, and dead bodies are everywhere. It looks as if at least three thousand men have been killed in some kind of battle. You think that an enemy must have come down and attacked your people. You are wrong. These people all turned against God and worshiped an idol.

As you help bury the dead, you keep looking for signs of your family. No one seems to know where they are. You hope they are all right. You search for your family's tent.

Finally, you see one in the distance with colorful decorations all over it. Only Mary and Mariah would decorate a tent like that. You run toward it. As you draw closer, you hear voices.

"If you save any manna overnight, it will turn into bugs," Mariah says.

"That's not true," Mary says. "That only happened to Naomi. What if I get hungry in the night?"

"Girls," your mother says in a stern tone. "Get rid of those pieces of honey-bread now. I will not have maggots living in our tent with us."

Mary exits the tent first and sees you. She gives a high-pitched squeal, which is soon joined by Mariah's screams. "You're back! You're back!"

You give them each a hug as your mother comes out of the tent to see what the commotion is. You hear a sob catch in her throat and then her arms wrap around you. Behind her, your father waits to greet you.

"We thought the Egyptians had killed you," your father says. He gives a bear hug around you and your mother when she refuses to let you go. You wipe tears from your eyes. When you are finally able to stand back and look at your family, you see that they have all grown thinner, and there are dark circles around your parents' eyes.

As Moses leaves to go up Mount Sinai again, you and your family spend a lot of time with each other. You tell your family about your experiences, and they tell you about everything you missed. The people made a covenant, a serious agreement, with God. Those who died had broken the covenant.

The God of Moses scares you. This God is even more powerful than you imagined, and deadly. Being with Haran was so much easier.

CHOICE ONE: If you stay with Israel, go to page 70.

CHOICE TWO: If you leave to find Haran, go to page 37.

You decide to go with your friends. As you wave goodbye to Caleb, you ask your friends, "Is snake hunting safe?"

"Sure," your friend says. "Eight of us are going. We'll bring home lots of meat so we don't have to eat manna all the time."

You hunt for days. Although you see a lot of snakes, none of you is quick enough to catch them. After days of unsuccessful snake hunting, you are all starving. On the last day, you almost get a snake with your knife before it coils up and hisses at you. You jump back. It strikes, but it only gets the air. As you run from it, you think, *That's it for me. Manna is better than this!* Your friends run back toward camp with you. The whole way, all you can think about is eating those sweet-tasting wafers.

By the time you reach the camp, Moses has returned, and it looks like all of Israel is getting ready to leave. Tents are being taken down; dogs are barking; sheep are bleating. A camel spits at you as you walk by it. You are glad to be home.

"You got back just in time," your father says. "How did the hunting go?"

"Don't ask," you say. Your father laughs.

Mary says, "You missed all the excitement."

"You should've seen what Moses looked like when he came down from the mountain," Mariah says. But the twins refuse to say anything else.

You help break camp for the big journey ahead to the Promised Land.

THE END

◆ ◆ ◆

Y_{ou} are so tired that you fall down by your family's things. Sand gets into your mouth. It is still warm from the day, but you are too tired even to spit it out. You feel the situation is hopeless. You shut your eyes.

Mariah says, "Mary, if I die, you may have my favorite blue bead."

"You just can't die," Mary wails. "If the Egyptians separate us, I'll always remember you. You are my best twin in the whole world."

"She's your only twin," you mutter into the sand just before you fall asleep. Someone pulls on your arm.

"Stop it!" you say. It's probably Mariah and Mary bugging you again. You turn over. The desert sand feels gritty against your skin.

"Get up now," your mother's voice says. It sounds far away. Someone keeps pulling your arm.

"I don't want to wake up just to die," you mumble.

Someone pinches your ear. "Ow!" You open one eyelid. Your mother is holding Kilion with one hand and your ear with the other. You cannot figure out what is going on. Your legs are heavy.

"We have to walk," she says, but her voice is distant. You would nod your head, but her fingers hold your earlobe in place.

"Just let me sleep a little more," you beg, wondering why the dream seems so real.

"Stop your complaining," she says. Your mother usually is not so demanding. This has to be a dream.

You follow her, or at least follow in the direction your ear is being pulled, because you do not have a choice. For being in the middle of a dream, your earlobe sure hurts, and your legs ache. You stub your toe on a rock and get dirt in your sandals. This dream journey seems to take forever. You are in some strange kind of tunnel or something like a tunnel, but the sky is still above you. Is that a fish you just saw swimming above your head on the left?

Maybe you are drowning.

"I don't know how to swim!" you yell. You feel a harder pinch on your earlobe. Then you feel hands tugging on your arms. Are the twins both trying to wake you up now? You seem to be going up a hill. Finally, the pressure on your ear is gone. You fall into a dreamless sleep.

A loud roaring sound wakes you up. All the people are crowded around you looking in the same direction. You stand up and see two huge waves crashing together on the sea, and are those chariot wheels? Suddenly, you realize that you are on the other side of the Red Sea from where you fell asleep.

"How did I get here?" you ask. The twins are giggling.

"You swam across," Mary teases.

"No, you really rode across on a crocodile's back," Mariah adds. "I was so frightened for you."

"Good one, Mariah," Mary says, patting her on the back.

"I liked yours, too," Mariah says.

"No more of these late nights for you," says your mother. "God opened the sea, and we all walked across."

You walked across the Red Sea. So the fish above you was not a dream. You wish you could remember it more clearly. Everyone is talking about the miracle God did for Israel. You can see dead Egyptian soldiers floating in the water. You realize that God just defeated the powerful and scary Egyptian army in a few moments. Seeing the force of that water, you are glad that you did not have to swim across.

Moses' sister, Miriam, starts singing a song of praise to the Lord.

Children and women dance along the edge of the sea, rejoicing that they are safe. You are so excited that you also start praising this God Moses has told everyone about, the one who calls Himself I AM. You choose to follow Him.

THE END

You look at the huge basket and feel embarrassed. You return it to the tent and get one that holds only an omer. You hand Kilion a piece of manna. He stuffs it into his mouth. He does not have teeth yet, but he gums at the manna, smiling. "Mmmm." His saliva drips down his face.

As you fill your basket, you taste the manna over and over. You try to figure out what it is made of, but the flavor is like nothing you have eaten before. It smells sweet and tastes a little like your mother's honey bread, only much better. It feels light and flaky.

From that day on, the manna comes every morning. You pick up only the amount that you will eat for that day, except on the day before the Sabbath. Then you collect enough for two days. Some people eat manna as it is, and others find all kinds of ways to fix it—manna cakes, manna crackers, manna burgers. It truly is an amazing food.

It is now three months since you left Egypt. You set up a camp near the base of Mount Sinai. It feels good to rest from traveling. Shortly after you arrive, you watch Moses start up the mountain to meet with God.

"Yeah, right," Esau says. "Like God lives on top of a mountain."

You laugh. "I think Moses said that God was going to meet him up there at the top."

"Well, good riddance," Esau says. "I'm tired of Moses telling us what to do all the time."

Mary and Mariah count the days that Moses has been gone. Life in camp becomes a dull routine.

"Moses has been gone thirty-three days," Mariah says one morning.

"No, I'm positive that he left thirty-eight days ago," says Mary.

You shrug. Moses has been gone a long, long time.

"He's probably dead," your father says slowly. You hope Moses is safe. If he is not, then what will happen to all of you? You look up at the cloud that hovers over the top of Mount Sinai.

Esau's father and some other men collect gold jewelry from the people. They want to make a god to worship like the ones the Egyptians had. They even ask your mother for her jewelry to melt down for their idol!

"Please don't give it to them," cries Mary. Mariah is sobbing so hard that she cannot speak. Mary continues, "Don't you love us? If you give that to them, what will we have for a dowry?"

Your mother rolls her eyes, but she refuses to give them her jewelry. The jewelry was from your Egyptian masters. They gave it to her just before you left Egypt. Esau's father and some of the other men talk Aaron into making a calf out of the gold they collected.

Once it is made, Esau runs over to you. "You're missing out on a good time!"

You shrug. "What's going on?"

"I'm going to give homage to the golden calf," Esau says. He looks excited.

"You're going to what?" you ask.

"It looks just like the god that Ramses had outside of his palace. Do you remember the one that we could just see from the top of the hill?" Esau says. "Now that's a god for you. That's the kind of god we should worship."

"You don't really believe that, do you?" you ask.

"Don't you?" Esau asks. "Come on. Moses is dead. It's time for us to get on with our lives. Are you coming?"

CHOICE ONE: If you refuse to worship the golden calf, go to page 59.

CHOICE TWO: If you go with Esau, go to page 43.

◆　◆　◆

Thinking does not help. You do not understand, but you know that what Esau and his father did was wrong. You find your father. He holds out his arms to you, and you rush into them, sobbing.

"I don't like it when people die," you say.

"I don't either," your father says.

"Why did Esau have to die?" you cry. Your father holds you in his arms, and you draw comfort from him.

After a while, your father says, "I don't know why Esau chose to rebel against God. I don't know why his father taught him to rebel. What I do know is that our God is God."

Your heart is heavy, but seeing how Esau ended up helps you make a decision. You will spend your life doing whatever God wants you to do. Even though you still grumble and complain sometimes on your long trip through the desert, you ask God for forgiveness when you do.

Forty years later, when you are fifty-two years old, you watch the swollen waters of the Jordan River part, and you remember how God made a path for you through the Red Sea when you were only a child. Your lifelong dream comes true. You cross the Jordan River into the Promised Land, the "land flowing with milk and honey." Mary, Mariah, and Kilion are glad to get there, too. But even at age fifty, Mary is afraid of the bees that make the honey.

THE END

"Please, may I ride with you?" you beg. You really do not want to be trampled by the other chariots.

"You'll slow me down," says your master.

"I'm light," you say. "Your horse will never know I'm here. Besides, a man who is as good a charioteer as you are won't even notice a little more weight. From what I saw yesterday, you must be the best charioteer in Pharaoh's army."

Your master smiles. "Well said, young one. Hop on for the ride of your life!"

You understand what he means when the chariot begins moving forward. The air rushes past you. The chariot feels like it is flying as it bumps over the sand. Your heart races. In your chest, you feel a kind of excitement that you have never felt before. You can hardly breathe. You grip the edge of the chariot.

In only moments, you have reached the Red Sea. You bump down into the seabed. The walls of water on either side tower over you. Even in your master's grand chariot, you feel small and unimportant.

"I've seen many things," your master yells back at you, "but never this. This God of Israel is great, but the gods of Egypt are greater."

"I'm not so sure about that," you say. You remember the plagues in Egypt. In the distance, you watch Moses pointing his staff at the sea from a cliff.

"Uh-oh," you say. The walls of water collapse.

The force of the water slams your head against the side of the chariot and buries you in the sea.

THE END

You decide that rocks are no match for swords. You stay hidden. From where you are perched, you can see that Moses has his hands up. Now and then, he lowers his arms—probably to let some blood flow back into them. Every time he does, Israel starts losing. When he lifts them up again, Israel pushes ahead.

After a while, you can tell that Moses is getting tired, because his arms are falling down more often. You panic. Someone needs to do something! Then Aaron, Moses' brother, and Hur, a leader of Israel, stand on either side of Moses and hold up his arms until sunset.

Israel wins, and you raise your arms like Moses and praise God. You feel sure that He will get you safely to the Promised Land. You cannot wait to taste the milk, honey, and all the wonderful foods there. Mariah says that rich food will be bad for her complexion. Mary is afraid of the bees that will make the honey. You are not afraid. God has been good to Israel. He chose the Promised Land for you. You choose to believe that it will be a wonderful place. You cannot wait to get there.

THE END

"Pharaoh's army is coming too fast!" you say to yourself. You are afraid that they will not notice that you are there. You change your mind and begin running back toward the Israelite camp. As you run, your eyes latch on to the pillar of cloud that God has used to guide Israel to the Red Sea. Suddenly, it is moving toward you. It stops directly between you and the Israelite camp. You can no longer smell the campfires.

"Oh no!" you yell. Your way back to camp is cut off. The Egyptian army is close behind you. You close your eyes and wait to be trampled to death.

Instead of being trampled, you hear chariot wheels grinding to a halt, horses whinnying in fear, and men shouting.

"Is it a sandstorm?" a loud voice asks.

"Can we get through it?" another yells. You open your eyes. No one seems to notice you. One Israelite child alone could not be much of a threat. You take a step away from them.

An important-looking officer says, "First line, forward." An entire section of chariots tries to move forward, but the horses will not get any nearer to the cloud. They back up no matter how hard their masters whip them.

One man jumps down from his chariot and charges right into the cloud with a battle cry. Everyone waits. And waits. And waits. The man never returns.

CHOICE ONE: If you run up to a soldier in one of the chariots and beg for mercy, go to page 75.

CHOICE TWO: If you try to run around the cloud, go to page 58.

You run all the next day. You are afraid that the Egyptians have already reached your family. If that is true, then you are all alone. You are the only Israelite who has survived the Egyptians. If your family is not dead, they are certainly slaves again. The thought brings you such sorrow that you begin to cry. Your eyes become blurred. You cannot tell where you are going anymore, so you stop, fall to your knees, and cover your face with your rough hands.

When you can cry no longer, you remove your hands and wipe your nose with your sleeve. In the distance you see a caravan. You feel an ache inside. You do not want to live the rest of your life alone. You run toward the caravan, hoping they are not a mirage. The gnawing pain in your stomach reminds you that you have not eaten solid food since you left your father's tent.

"Please, kind travelers," you yell once you are within range, "I wish to go with you, wherever you are going."

A man with twinkling eyes and a ready smile says, "We are traders headed for the Far East."

"Are you really?" you ask. When you were a slave, you would see exotic travelers passing by but never dreamed that you would be able to travel with them and see the rest of the world. You have always wondered what lies beyond Egypt.

"You look like a sturdy traveler." The caravan leader smiles.

You stand up taller. "I am. I would like to join your caravan. I will work, of course."

"Good. We are in need of workers."

Over the years as you journey with these merchants, you see many amazing sights. Every once in a while, you hear rumors about how God saved His people, the Israelites, from the Egyptians. You wonder if the rumors are true and if you should have stayed with them. You will never know.

THE END

Where will you find food? Where will you find water? For three days, you wander with the rest of Israel. Blisters swell on your feet and make you limp. Your meals are getting smaller and smaller. Your growling stomach makes you grumpy, and the twins are annoying you with their complaining.

"I'm hungry. My stomach huuuurts!" Mary says, stretching out the last word for effect. Mariah is upset because the shine has left her hair.

At a place called Marah you find water, but your hopes are dashed. It is too bitter to drink.

"It's all Moses' fault," Esau's father complains. Everyone grumbles.

You join them. "Moses, why did you lead us out into the desert to die of thirst?"

You watch Moses ask God about it. Then Moses throws a stick into the water. It turns the water sweet. You guzzle the cool water, letting some spill on your face and drip down your neck. You feel a little hopeful. Moses solved the water problem for now, but when will he solve the food problem?

"This isn't how I pictured the journey to the Promised Land," Esau says.

"We'll die of starvation or foot sores before we get there," you say.

Your parents seem to be taking things pretty well.

"One thing at a time," your father says. Your mother nods her head in agreement and tries to comfort you, your brother, and your sisters. But every now and then you see worry lines in her face.

One day Esau's father says, "We ate our last food this morning. Moses brought us into the wilderness to die."

The whole camp is saying the same thing. "Why didn't we just die in Egypt?"

Then Moses tells everyone, "God will send food from the sky."

Can you believe him?

"This evening you will have meat," Moses continues. "In the morning God will rain bread from the sky. Take only as much as you can eat for the day. On the day before the Sabbath, gather enough for two days."

That evening, thousands of quail cover the camp. The birds are easily caught. You help your mom pluck and roast the birds. You stuff yourself and go to bed full for the first time since you can remember. You dream of cows, birds, leeks, and melons falling from the sky. One cow falls onto your tent, right on top of you. You wake up. It was not a cow. The twins are jumping on you.

"What are you doing?" you demand.

"You've got to come and see what God sent for breakfast," Mariah says. "I don't know if it'll be good for my figure or not, but it really tastes good."

"It's sweet like honey," Mary says. "And there are no bees."

Your sisters hurry out of the tent. You sit up and squint at the bright light coming through the flaps.

You get dressed and go outside. Covering the ground are thin flakes of something white. People everywhere are gathering them.

Your sisters are collecting the white flakes. This mysterious food goes into their mouths as well as their baskets. You pick up a flake and taste it. Your eyes open wide. It is delicious. It is like a sweet cracker or bread. You have never tasted anything like it.

Mary calls, "Mother, Mariah and I each have an omer. Can we go play now?"

"Go ahead," your mother says. She turns to you. "Collect only as much manna as you can eat today. I'll get enough for Kilion, your father, and me."

"Okay," you say. You grab a great big basket. You have a really large appetite.

Moses calls out to remind people, "Take only what you need. Do not save any until morning."

CHOICE ONE: If you do what Moses says,
go to page 23.

CHOICE TWO: If you ignore Moses and take all you
want, go to page 78.

◆ ◆ ◆

The God of Moses frightens you. The burning mountain that others call Sinai is scary. What if the fire should leave the top and attack the ground where your tents are? Although you are glad to be with other Israelites, they are not how you remembered them.

"This stinks," someone said the first day you were back.

"What stinks?" you asked. You sniffed the air thinking he meant the smoke from the mountain.

"Living like this," he said.

Several days later, you look around you. Everyone has a place to stay. God provides manna for people to eat every morning. No foreign army is attacking. What are these people complaining about? They seem to have everything! Do they want to go back to Egypt? You do not! Have they forgotten what it was like being slaves? You are tired of listening to all their complaints.

Mary groans, "How much longer must we live like this?"

"That's enough!" you say. You almost wish Haran had never found the Israelite camp. Your heart longs for his merry ways.

"What's your problem?" Mariah asks.

"You and the others complain all the time," you say. "Yet you have everything you need. Traveling with Haran's caravan was tough, but his people stayed pleasant."

"Touchy, touchy," says Mariah.

"And if there was a dangerous mountain with fire on it, Haran wouldn't be camping by it," you say.

"Are you scared?" asks Mary. She begins to taunt, "Scaredy-cat! Scaredy-cat!"

The rest of the day, you compare Haran's camp to Israel's camp. Later that night, you tell your father, "I want to go east and find Haran."

He shakes his head. "You would leave the God of Israel?"

"I want to leave the grumbling and complaining," you say. "I don't know what is going on here with fire on the mountain, but I want to leave."

When you leave your family, everyone cries, including you, but leaving the other Israelites is not hard at all. You head east. You never find Haran's caravan. The next caravan owner you meet is not so nice. You become his slave for life.

THE END

The Egyptians are waiting for you on the other side of the pillar of cloud. No one knows when or where the pillar will move, and danger lurks behind it.

What am I doing sitting here? you think. *I've got to get across that sea before tomorrow.*

You ask your parents, "Can you teach me how to swim?"

"I don't know how," your mother says as she holds your sleeping brother to her chest.

Your father shakes his head. "When would we have had the chance to learn? The Egyptians kept us working so hard, we didn't have time. Besides, swimming in crocodile-infested waters didn't really appeal to me."

You laugh nervously. You go and ask another family camped near yours, "Do you know how to swim?" They do not know either. You go to the next family and then the next.

Most of the adults are packing up to leave. They do not have time to spend talking to you.

"Why do you want to swim?" one man asks, not really expecting an answer.

You turn away. The pillar is lighting up the whole camp, and it hardly seems like night. Finally, you give up trying to find a swimming teacher and stumble toward where your family is camped.

CHOICE ONE: If you stay awake the rest of the night, go to page 63.

CHOICE TWO: If you go to sleep, go to page 20.

"Go have fun," you say. "I'll just hang out here." Esau leaves, and you stay where you are and watch. The crowd in front of the golden calf looks too rowdy to be safe. Besides, you do not want your parents getting more upset with you. You have not been getting along with them very well lately. You watch for quite a while. The people look like little children dancing around the calf.

Suddenly, you see Moses coming down the mountain. He smashes some stone tablets on the rocks and looks really angry. He grabs the golden calf and grinds it to powder with some rocks. Then he spreads the powder on the water. He makes everyone drink some, even you. It makes you gag. As you are choking, you hear Moses ask Aaron why he did it.

"It wasn't my fault!" Aaron says. "The people didn't know what happened to you. You know how easily they slip back into doing evil."

Moses did not look convinced.

"I only asked them to take off their gold jewelry. Then I threw it into the fire, and out popped this golden calf."

Oh brother! you think. You cannot believe that Aaron is telling such a whopper of a lie. I guess that's what happens when you listen to the wrong people.

You are going to stay away from people who disobey God from now on. It is not worth it. You clear the last particles of that horrible gold from your throat and decide that you will never worship any god except the real God.

THE END

◆ ◆ ◆

The dust is flying up around Pharaoh's army.

How will they be able to see you? Thinking quickly, you untie the white cloth from your head and wave it with all your might. Your waving arms make a cool breeze around you. You stand on your tiptoes to make yourself taller. Surely the white cloth will get the attention of Pharaoh's lead charioteers.

You glance back at the Israelite camp. They look so far away. You turn back to watch Pharaoh's chariots. They are bearing down on you. They are traveling so fast. They do not even slow down! You are able to dodge one by jumping to the side. You roll out of the path of another. Unfortunately, you roll directly into the path of the horse pulling the next chariot. You are trampled to death.

THE END

◆ ◆ ◆

You are tired from running. You turn around and head back to the campsite. Your efforts have been in vain, and you are exhausted. How will you ever have the strength to continue looking for a crossing? Tears stream down your face. You want to help, but you have not been able to do anything.

At first light, you reach what should have been the camp, but no one is there. Just then, you see someone by the Red Sea. You hurry to the edge.

"Wait," you cry. "Where is everyone?"

You are amazed at what you see. It looks like there is a canyon of dry land right down the middle of the Red Sea. You can smell the fish. Some people are running along the bottom. How can this be happening? You see figures way in the distance on the opposite bank. It's hard to tell who they are, but you think that it must be the Israelites. The runners are getting close to the other shore. You have to catch up!

You take a deep breath. You cannot figure out what is keeping the water from splashing down on you. You hear a noise behind you. God's pillar of cloud is lifting. The Egyptian chariots are heading toward you. Your heart is beating wildly.

CHOICE ONE: If you go back and run along the seaside from which you came, go to page 74.

CHOICE TWO: If you turn and run harder into the middle of the Red Sea, go to page 50.

"It's just jewelry in the shape of a baby cow," you say. "Don't give me that god stuff."

"Come on," Esau says. "We're just trying to have some fun."

I'm sure everyone is tired and bored like I am, you think. *I'm sure they all know the calf isn't really God.* The more you think about what they are doing, the less you see wrong with it. They are not really hurting anything, not really. You see that your parents are not looking. You sneak away with Esau.

Some people are remaining in their tents. When you reach the area where the golden calf is standing, you see people everywhere. A lot of the women are wearing clothes that belonged to the Egyptians. They do not cover their bodies as well as they should. The men are just as bad. They have made something to drink, which is making them act very silly. You wonder how grown people can behave so foolishly.

"Come on," Esau says. He pushes his way through to the front of the pack and bows low before the golden calf. You look around you. You wish you were anywhere but here.

From his position on the ground, he says, "Don't embarrass me. Bow down. Everyone will think you're an ally of Moses if you don't worship our new god."

You give the golden image an awkward bow and then hurry away. The next day it is not as hard to bow down, and the following day, you bow all the way to the ground. Of course you and Esau laugh about it later, as if acting silly in front of a golden calf is not a big deal.

Then one day, Moses returns. The glow on his face frightens you. He looks really angry. He destroys the golden calf, and many die by the sword for worshiping it and leading people the wrong way.

It is not until you are dying of a plague—a painful illness—a few days later that you realize how horrible you were acting. You were unfaithful to the real God. Now you are paying for your terrible sin. You ask God for forgiveness before you die.

THE END

When you return to your family's tent, your father comes out to meet you.

"Moses killed my friend," you yell. "How could he? Why did God save us from Egypt to kill us here?"

Your father holds you close to him. "Moses didn't kill anyone. The sons of Levi fought against everyone who chose an idol instead of the living God. Esau and his father cursed God and said they would rather die."

"That's not what they meant," you say, pounding your hands against your father's chest. You cannot control your tears as they course down your cheeks. "I won't believe in a God who kills kids. I won't. I won't."

"God didn't want them to die," your father said. "They chose death over obedience to Him."

You refuse to listen. From that day forward, you disobey the laws of God whenever you get the chance. You have an unhappy life. You die of a snakebite in the desert when you are thirty-five.

THE END

You decide that you need to do something to help Israel. You pick up a few rough stones and hurry closer to the battlefield. You see an enemy soldier below you. Sweat trickles down your back as you wait for him to get closer to where you are hiding. When he is close enough, you throw a stone, but it misses his head. He looks in your direction. You throw another stone. It hits his shoulder just as an Israelite soldier comes up behind him. Yes!

Suddenly, you hear someone behind you. You look over your shoulder. It is an Amalekite. You grab another stone and throw it as hard as you can. It hits him on the side of the head. He pauses, but the rock does not stop him. He darts toward you.

CHOICE ONE: If you shout for help, go to page 12.

CHOICE TWO: If you drop to the ground and roll toward the man's legs, go to page 61.

You know you will be in the way. You do not want to be trampled by the horses, so you hurriedly weave your way in and out of chariots until you are able to reach the back of the army where the servants are. You breathe a sigh of relief when you reach them.

"You are Baala's new slave?" asks a man who keeps his nose high in the air. You nod warily.

"I am Baala's head servant," he says. "From now on, you will take orders from me. Call me 'Your Highness.' Do you understand, slave?"

You nod but do not say anything. The man keeps talking and talking and talking about what you have to do. There must be more rules at Baala's house than in all the rest of Egypt! You nod every now and then while he talks, but you keep your eyes on the charioteers. They are a mighty army, probably the strongest in the world. You almost feel a sense of pride at being Baala's slave. Serving a powerful person like him will have its benefits. When the Egyptians return home with the Israelites, you will beg for your family's lives.

The servant keeps talking, but you no longer pay attention. Far in the distance, you see that the entire Egyptian army has entered the opening in the Red Sea. Suddenly, without warning, the sea closes in over the Egyptians with a crashing wave.

"Oh no!" you say as others around you begin shrieking. A few of the servants run toward the Red Sea. The slaves run in the opposite direction. You notice that the head servant with all of the rules is running away with the slaves.

At that moment, you cannot help but say, "Moses' God is God. He saved all of Israel."

You start running toward the Red Sea. The thick sand cannot keep you from your task. You want to find a way around the sea. You want to be with Israel and their God; a God as powerful as this deserves your loyalty.

It takes many days to find a way around the sea. For ten years, you wander in the desert looking for your family. You get really tired of eating locusts. Finally, one morning you wake behind a sand dune to find a white flaky substance all over the ground. You are examining it when someone comes over the dune with a basket.

"Mariah!" you shout. She drops her basket and runs to you.

You have never been so happy to see anyone before. You join your family in the Israelite camp and serve the God of Israel for the rest of your life.

THE END

You take a deep breath and sprint down the Red Sea path toward the other side. You are tired, but you have never run as fast as you are running now. No matter what happens, you do not want to be left behind. Your lungs burn as you race to catch up with your family. Most of the other Israelites are already on the other shore. You hear the thunder of hooves and the rattle of chariots behind you.

You try to get more air into your lungs, but you can hardly breathe. You push yourself forward with long strides. Your feet pound the dry earth beneath you. Just four more steps. Now three.

Suddenly the wind roars, and you sense the wall of water falling. Two more steps. The shore is a blur in front of you. You strain to reach it, but you feel water splashing your legs. You are being swept away!

"Help!" you call out but know that it is too late. Then you feel a strong hand grabbing your arm. The next thing you know, your father has pulled you from the water. You are safe! You hug your father, laughing and crying at the same time. You do not want to leave the safety of his arms.

After a praise celebration to thank God, you continue your travels to the Promised Land. For weeks, you and the other Israelites travel under the scorching desert sun. You wish you had your house in Egypt to protect you. God sends you manna, bread from the sky, to eat every day, but you miss the cool, juicy melons and cucumbers of past meals.

Lots of people are missing Egypt, just as you are. You are not used to traveling like this.

"Let's go find something else to eat," Esau says one morning. When your parents give you permission, you both go hunting with a group of others.

After you find nothing, the leader of the group says, "We could go back to camp if anyone knows where it is."

"What?" exclaims Esau. "Are we lost?" The leader nods his head. As you search for your families, you go an entire week without food.

"What's that in the distance?" you ask one day.

"It's our families!" cries your leader. Even in your weakened condition, you all run as fast as you can to the camp. From then on, manna tastes pretty good.

Soon, you camp in front of a mountain called Sinai. God talks to Moses. Then Moses consecrates the people. He sets you all apart as holy for God. You feel really clean on the inside. The next day, you help wash your family's clothes so you will also be clean on the outside and ready to meet with God. By the time you are through, your hands feel raw.

The third morning, thunder is crashing and lightning slits the sky. The mountain has a thick cloud over it, and you hear a loud trumpet blast.

"What's that?" you ask, trying to cover the fact that your teeth are chattering.

"I hope we don't have to stand and listen to more people talking," Mary says.

"Mariah and Mary, stop talking like that," your father says. "Have you no fear of God?"

They look ashamed. Moses leads everyone to the base of the mountain. All but Moses must stay off the holy mountain or die.

Going up the mountain is not even a temptation for you. Smoke billows from Mount Sinai like smoke from a blazing furnace. The whole mountain is shaking as if it will erupt or split apart at any moment. Even though you are standing at a distance with the rest of the crowd, you want to turn and run. Moses actually starts up the mountain to talk with God! You are afraid to look. He will probably be burned alive.

Soon, Moses comes down. Somehow he survived the dangerous mountain. He tells everyone what God said. "Do not make for yourselves gods of silver or gold." He tells you lots of other things God said, including that He will make your enemies run in fear. Then God calls Aaron and seventy-two others to the mountain to worship at a distance.

Later, Moses tells the people about God's words and laws. Everyone agrees, saying, "Everything the Lord has said we will do."

God calls Moses up the mountain again. Aaron and Hur are left in charge. As you watch Moses enter the dark cloud, you wonder if you will ever see him again.

You think, *No human could live through the raging fire on the top of the mountain!*

Moses is barely gone before people start complaining. Aaron looks like he wants to run away from it all, too. The complaining builds week after week as Moses fails to return.

Esau says, "Moses isn't coming back, and now we're stuck here in the desert. I wish we were back in Egypt."

Another friend says, "Do you remember the wonderful things we had there?"

Your mother shakes her head and pulls you aside. "I don't want you hanging around Esau and his group of friends."

CHOICE ONE: If you obey your mother, go to page 14.

CHOICE TWO: If you hang around with your friends anyway, go to page 72.

You turn around and go north. As you stand at the edge of the sea, you question what you saw. Did it really happen? Shattered chariots and the bodies of horses and men on the shore take away your doubts. You stare across the sea but detect no one. Tears sting your eyes.

You walk farther north. You are so thirsty and tired that eventually you fall facedown on the ground, expecting never to wake up. You feel the sand gradually covering you like a grave. When you regain consciousness, cold water is being poured on your face. You drink in as much as you can.

Only after you have had your fill do you say, "Who are you? What are you doing?"

"So the dead comes back to life," says a strange man with a fiery jewel on his turban. He helps you sit up. His colorful robes make you dizzy. He offers you another drink.

"There, that's better. Bring the child some food," he calls, clapping his hands. You eat some kind of brown mush in a bowl. You do not care what it is. You gulp it down as quickly as you can get it into your mouth. Only when you are done do you remember your manners and say, "Thank you." The man laughs at your poor attempt at politeness.

"I am Haran," says the man. "Little Pilgrim, what are you doing out here in the desert all by yourself?"

"I was with Moses and all my people," you say, "but the Egyptian army came after us."

"You mean the powerful army of Pharaoh?"

"Yes. Pharaoh let us go, but then he sent his army after us. God held back the sea, and everyone crossed through, and then the water fell on all the Egyptians and killed them."

Haran laughs. "If you do not want to tell me the truth, just say so."

"But I am telling you the truth," you say.

He looks surprised. "Then why are you here?" he asks.

You hang your head. "I was trying to find a way across the sea so my family could escape. I got back too late."

Haran looks at you with pity in his eyes. "I do not know if I believe your story, but many things happen that I do not understand." He fingers the jewel on his turban. "It is difficult to get along in this world without family. You may travel with us if you like."

CHOICE ONE: If you go with Haran, turn to page 67.

CHOICE TWO: If you ask him to help you to the other side of the sea so you can find your family, go to page 16.

The party does look like lots of fun. What difference will it make? You will be careful. You stand up.

"Lead the way," you say.

You join the others around the golden calf. You feel a little guilty at first, but then you really get into it. Someone gives you a drink that makes you feel light-headed and dizzy. You bow down and worship the idol. Then you join in all the fun, laughing and carrying on any way you like.

After a while, you see Moses storming toward you. He grabs the calf. You do not care. You and your friends keep partying. Moses makes you drink something that tastes awful, but you follow it with more good food and drink. You do not even notice what is going on around you until you hear a loud voice shouting.

"Whoever is for the Lord, come to me." It is Moses. You and your friends just stand there.

"Who is he to come back and spoil all our fun?" Esau says.

You all agree and go back to your party. Suddenly, you realize that men with swords are killing lots of the people. One kills Esau. Then he kills you.

THE END

"No, you go ahead," you say. "I'm going to stay around here."

"You can't tell me that you want to eat more manna," Esau exclaims.

You shrug. "It's not that bad. Have fun, and get a snake for me."

As your friends leave, Caleb turns to you. "I'm glad you didn't go. Moses has been gone on the mountain for forty days and nights. It's the second time he has been gone that long." You both gaze up at the fiery mountaintop.

"Do you think he's still alive?" you ask.

"He's alive," Caleb says with a smile.

Just then, you see someone coming out of the cloud. It is Moses. He is carrying stone tablets. When you see his face, you and Caleb pull back in fear. Moses looks as though his whole face is lit up like lightning.

You both run back to the camp. Aaron and the others are afraid too. Finally, Moses calls to all of you. First the leaders go toward him. They look like they could turn and run at any second. When they reach Moses, he talks to them. Finally, everyone finds the courage to go up to Moses. He shows you what God wrote on the tablets. Then he tells you all the commands that God gave him for Israel. One of them is not to eat snakes.

As you listen to Moses, everything makes sense. It is good to tell the truth and to obey your parents.

You think, *Why would I want to worship any god but the God of Israel? Who else has such power and such wisdom?*

When Moses is finished, he puts a veil over his face. From that time on, after every visit Moses has with God, his face glows, and he covers it with a veil.

What a wonderful God Israel has! His light shines so brightly that Moses' face shows it too. You decide that you will follow your God all of your days. You have a good and exciting life.

THE END

While everyone is waiting for the warrior's return, you begin to back up and then start running away from the chariots, horses, and fierce-looking soldiers. You run as fast as you can, not looking over your shoulder for fear that you are being followed.

You run and run, but the cloud does not seem to end. It is completely protecting the Israelites. God has kept His promise just like Moses said He would. He is protecting His people.

You hear chariot wheels moving behind you, and an Egyptian soldier yells, "Stop, slave!"

Having him so close scares you. You keep running. The last thing you remember is the pain of an arrow piercing your back. You fall forward, dead.

THE END

"No. I don't believe that melted earrings and necklaces can make a god," you say. "Pharaoh's idols didn't protect his army at the Red Sea. Grow up, Esau."

"I don't care what you say. Moses and his God are dead. Now we have a real god."

"Talk about dead! That golden calf isn't alive. It has no power at all."

"You're no fun anymore," Esau says. He walks away from you.

"You did the right thing," your mother says, coming out from the tent. "There's only one God, and that calf isn't it."

Mary and Mariah have been listening, and Mary pleads, "Mother, you don't understand. All our friends are over there. Can't we go, too?"

"No, you stay here with us."

Mariah stamps her foot, "But all our friends will think we're weird."

"Let them think what they want. This family will not have any part of idol worship. Is that clear? Stay on this side of the camp."

You try to hide your smile.

"Oh, all right," they mutter together.

A few days later as you are munching on a baked manna snack, your father runs into the tent. "Moses is back, and he is furious."

"I didn't do anything," Mariah says.

"She didn't, and I was with her the whole time," Mary adds. You laugh, but when you see the seriousness of your father's eyes, you stop.

"I want everyone to stay here for a while," your father says. "Don't leave this tent unless I come and get you."

You stay inside, but you can smell something burning. Later you hear yelling and the clanking of metal. When the noise is over, you learn that more than three thousand people were killed for turning their backs on God.

"Where's Esau?" you ask. Your father shakes his head. You continue, "Does that mean you don't know where he is?"

"It means," your father says slowly, "that Esau and his father are dead."

"No!" you cry.

You are angry with Moses and God because your friend died. Your father tries to comfort you, but you pull away. You go off by yourself to think.

CHOICE ONE: If you stay angry with Moses and God, go to page 46.

CHOICE TWO: If you trust God even though you are still confused by Esau's death, go to page 26.

You drop to the ground and ignore the stones digging into your ribs. You close your eyes and roll toward the man's legs to trip him. He loses his balance and falls on his sword right beside you. You feel his weight pressing against you. When you open your eyes, his blade is only two inches from your face. You are afraid to move.

The enemy soldier is dead. You gasp for air but do not feel as though you are getting enough. There is blood everywhere. You pass out.

You wake up when the battle is over. Esau finds you. He sneaked out of camp to make sure you were okay. He helps you walk home, and you tell him about everything that happened. Israel won the battle, and you are so grateful to be alive!

THE END

You are exhausted but choose to meet your doom with your eyes open. On your way to your family's tent, you stumble near the shore. The water looks deep. You dip your hand in, and a shiver runs up your arm and down your back. You give up on the idea of swimming across. A light breeze is blowing. In the distance, you see that Moses has raised his staff and stretched his hand out over the water. The breeze changes to a strong east wind.

Something really strange is happening over near Moses. Waves have risen on the sea, but they are going in opposite directions, some to the left and the rest to the right! You give in to curiosity and move closer to Moses.

There seems to be a shallow trench forming down the middle of the sea, all the way across to the other shore. You pull your cloak tightly around your body against the wind and try to protect your ears. The wind and waves are so loud that you would not be able to hear someone shouting right beside you.

The channel is getting deeper. A misty spray fills the air. Every now and then splashing water threatens to drench you. You move back, but not far enough. A wave slaps the side of the shore and drenches your legs. Again you back up. Water squishes in your sandals. As the trench deepens, the water on either side of it piles up like walls holding the rest of the sea back.

"So that's it!" you say to yourself. "God is making a path for us through the water." Then it dawns on you. God is in charge of the wind and the clouds. He is even in charge of the Red Sea.

You run back to your family. "Mary! Mariah! Come see!" The

girls must not have been sleeping soundly, for they both jump up at once.

"What is it? Are the Egyptians here?" Mary asks. "Oh, what will we do?"

"Don't be silly. Do you hear anyone screaming?" you ask.

Mariah calms down first. "Tell us what's happening."

"You won't believe until you see it. Follow me."

Just then your parents get up. "Hold it one minute, you three," your father says. "Help us break camp. Then you can go see whatever it is."

As you help pack your family's belongings, you keep glancing toward the sea. A crowd has started to gather near it. Finally, you and your sisters are free to go. You race over to the water's edge, dodging around people, animals, and belongings. When you arrive, you see that the trench now goes all the way down to the seabed. Instead of the muddy bottom that should be there, you see only a dry path through the sea.

"Yes!" you yell into the air as others also shout for joy. Mary and Mariah have caught up. Your father is not far behind. They join in the celebration, hugging and cheering. No one celebrates long, though. People at the front of the group grab their belongings and run toward the passage in the sea.

"Let's get your mother, the baby, and our things," your father shouts.

"But I'm scared!" Mary says. You hate it when she whines.

"What if the water caves in on us?" Mariah asks. Looking at the towering water walls, you think she has a point.

"Mary and Mariah, there's no time for your dramatics," your dad says. "We're going to walk straight through that sea, because God has opened the way for us."

As you help your mother pack the final few blankets, she keeps repeating, "It's unbelievable!"

Esau's father yells back, "What's so unbelievable? These windstorms happen all the time. It's just a fluke. We need to hurry before the wind changes, though."

Mariah rolls her eyes at you. "He doesn't make sense. The wind couldn't do that by itself." You agree.

You help steady the cart as your father pushes it down to the seabed. The ground is solid and dry.

"Don't look up!" you hear Mariah say. Mary is trembling, staring at the monumental walls of water. Mariah is pulling her along. At first, you feel closed in. You just want to run back to the shore and forget this whole thing.

Your mind keeps asking, *What is holding the water up?* After you have gone about a third of the way through the sea, you look back. You wonder, *What if the water starts falling in on me? Can I make it to the shore in time?* You wonder about this God who has called your people out of Egypt. Will He really protect you? You look at the wall of water on your right. Do you dare touch it? You can see fish swimming. Timidly, you reach out and touch the water. It feels cool and wet.

"The wind didn't do this," you say aloud. "God did it." You smile. Joy fills your heart. You help your father push the cart the rest of the way.

By the time you get across, you are hungry and extremely tired. Everyone is praising God. Women are singing and dancing with tambourines, but your eyes will not stay open another minute. You find a place to curl up and take a nap.

When you wake up, Esau is watching you. "How can you just sleep? Aren't you even hungry?"

"I suppose," you say.

"You think that just because we made it across the sea in a crazy windstorm that everything is fine?" he asks.

"What's wrong?" You rub your eyes and try to wake up completely.

"Where's the food?" Esau asks. "Where will we find food? We'll run out soon. I don't see any leeks or melons growing here. We'll starve in this desert." He stomps away from you.

CHOICE ONE: If you listen to Esau, go to page 34.

CHOICE TWO: If you ignore what he says,
go to page 80.

"Thank you," you say. "I would appreciate traveling with you."

Before long, you learn different things that you can do to make Haran's life easier. You are happy to serve him because he is generous and very rich.

"I will be sad when you leave," Haran says.

"I don't have to go," you say. You like traveling with this nice man.

"Would you like to be one of my servants?" Haran asks.

"I would," you say. You know that Haran is getting older and probably does not need another servant. He is just being nice.

He smiles at you. "You will be my personal servant. I am making one last trip before I settle down and retire."

"I will go with you wherever you go," you say.

"When we have finished trading our goods on this trip," Haran says, "I plan to come back this way and settle in a city called Jericho. It has good strong walls and will be a safe place."

You smile. Life is so full of adventures. You miss your family, but you feel sure they are safe somewhere. Soon you settle in Jericho with Haran. You have a good life there for the next forty years.

THE END

It seems impossible that God can protect you from the Egyptians forever, even though He did bring plagues against Pharaoh and Egypt. Watching them try to chase frogs from their homes was pretty funny. You smile.

God has done so much for you already. What else can He do? Maybe Pharaoh's army will be crushed by a stampeding herd of wild camels. Or a sandstorm could bury them.

How He does what He does is none of my business, you think. *The God who got me out of Egypt can keep me safe if He wants to.* Your brain hurts from thinking. You decide to get some rest. You sleep peacefully until the sound of a ram's horn wakens you a few hours before dawn.

"Moses has given the order to break camp," your father says.

"Where are we going?" you ask.

"I don't know," your father says, "but look at what's happening to the Red Sea."

You cannot believe your eyes. The water of the sea has dammed up into walls on both sides. There is a path through the middle of the sea! People are beginning to walk across it to the other bank.

"Mother!" you call. "Come and look." She joins you at the tent's entrance. Wind blows through the opening into the tent.

"Oh, no! Help me!" cries Mariah.

You run to her. "What's wrong?"

"The wind is ruining my hair," she says.

You almost tell her that the wind could not make it look any worse than sleeping on it has.

Mary rubs her eyes as she stares out at the Red Sea. "I'm not going through there. What if the water falls and drowns us?"

Quickly, you help your father and sisters break everything down and pack up. You are so excited that God has given you an escape route. Your whole family walks through the sea together. Even as you travel with high water on either side of you, it feels more like a dream than reality. No matter how long you live, you will never forget the fishy smell of being in the middle of the Red Sea.

Once all of Israel is across, God looses the water on the chariots of the pursuing Egyptians. Soon the dead bodies of your former masters line the shore. You praise God with the rest of Israel.

After several weeks of travel in the desert, Israel again comes face-to-face with an enemy. A people called the Amalekites come out to attack. You hope that God will save your people again, just as He did at the Red Sea.

Moses sends Joshua and others to meet the Amalekites in a valley. The battle seems to go on for so long. You just have to know what is happening. As an excuse to see the action, you get water to bring to Moses. You see him standing on a high hill watching the battle. You cannot get close enough to give him the water, so you drink it instead and hide behind a boulder.

Some of the fighting moves right below you. There are several loose rocks by your feet. Maybe you can use them as weapons.

CHOICE ONE: If you just watch the battle,
go to page 28.

CHOICE TWO: If you join the battle, go to page 47.

"No, I'm going to stay," you tell yourself. "I like the people with Haran better, but only here can I learn to serve the one true God."

"Who are you talking to?" Mary asks.

"Just myself," you say.

"You're weird," says Mariah. They both walk off, and all you can do is shake your head after them.

You do not let them stop you from talking, because you need to sort this out. "The God of Moses has saved my life and the lives of my family. It's enough for me just to know that He is God."

With that decided, you gather your manna for the day and then wander off toward Mount Sinai. You know it is forbidden to touch the mountain, but you want to get a little closer. You are curious about this God of Moses. As you near the base of the mountain, you notice someone looking up at it. It is no one you know.

You walk toward him. "See anything?"

"No," says the man. He turns to you. "You're Jacob's child aren't you, the one who was stuck on the wrong side of the sea?"

You laugh. "That's me."

"I'm Caleb," he says.

"It's pretty scary-looking up there, isn't it?" you say.

Caleb turns around and sits on a rock. "There's a good reason for that. Our God is mightier than anything we can imagine."

"I know. I tried to run away from Him at the Red Sea."

"I don't believe that you can hide from God," Caleb says. He spends a lot of time telling you about what God told Moses. You like

Caleb. He is closer to your father's age, but he talks to you as though you are an adult. And not once does he complain.

"There you are," Esau says. He, Ruth, Jaben, and some others come up behind you.

"We're tired of manna. Want to go snake hunting with us?"

CHOICE ONE: If you go snake hunting, go to page 19.

CHOICE TWO: If you stay with Caleb, go to page 56.

◆ ◆ ◆

Even though your parents told you not to, you hang around with your usual crowd.

"It's so hot," Ruth says.

"I'm tired of Moses telling us what to do," Jaben says.

"I can't wait to get out of this desert and eat something besides manna," you say.

Most of the time, you are either listening to people complaining or you are grumbling yourself. Many of the people think Moses is dead. He has been on the burning mountain too long.

"Aaron, we want you to make us a new god," some say.

You wonder if that would be right. *Can people really make whatever god they want?* you wonder. Those who are asking for a god are fun to be around, and they seem to know so much more than you.

"We want gods like the Egyptians have," they cry. "Make us gods to lead us!" You join in their demand for gods you can see instead of one you cannot.

Aaron finally agrees. He collects gold jewelry from the people. Then he takes a tool and forms a golden idol in the shape of a calf.

The people are excited. "Look at our god who brought us up out of Egypt!" they shout.

You like being able to see your god. This god is pretty. It is made of shiny, valuable gold. Aaron builds an altar to the new god. He calls for a holiday the next day. Your parents are really upset about it.

"Don't go near that calf," your father says.

"It's evil," adds your mother. "This is not why God delivered us from Egypt."

"Don't worry about me," you say. "I'm just watching because I'm bored. I'm not touching it. Looking can't hurt."

"Don't go near it," your mother says.

The next morning many, many people get up early to celebrate. You watch from a distance. They offer sacrifices to the golden calf. Then they eat, drink, and do lots of things that you know are not right. You begin to wonder if you should even be watching.

Esau sees you and waves. "What are you doing way over there?"

"Just watching," you say.

"Why are you watching when you could be having fun?" Esau asks.

CHOICE ONE: If you hang back and continue watching, go to page 40.

CHOICE TWO: If you join the party in front of the golden calf, go to page 55.

CHOICE THREE: If you walk away, go to page 82.

You do not want to be caught by the Egyptians, but water standing straight up in the air makes you nervous. You run back in the direction you came, down the shoreline. At least you know what to expect along this beach. You run until you realize that the Egyptians are not chasing you.

Only then do you stop and turn around. All the Egyptian chariots have moved into the path through the Red Sea. You pray to the God of Moses to protect your family.

Just then, you hear a roar. In a moment, the path that was dry is completely filled with water. You blink, trying to take in what you just saw. You stand there, unmoved for some time, watching the wild waves where the Egyptian army once was.

"I can't believe what I just saw," you say to yourself. You cannot take your eyes from the spot. Israel's God is so powerful that He wiped out all the Egyptian charioteers in a single stroke.

The idea of a God being that powerful scares you. The Egyptians' gods did not have that much power. What if Moses' God wants to kill you for not trusting Him? You plan to run away as far as you can. You do not want God to notice you, but where can you hide? You cannot go west or you will end up back in Egypt. You cannot go east because of the Red Sea. Perhaps you will find a trade route if you go north. Maybe you should go south and try to find someone with a boat to take you across.

CHOICE ONE: If you go south, go to page 77.

CHOICE TWO: If you go north, go to page 53.

♦ ♦ ♦

Y ou look at the faces of the soldiers in each chariot. They are fierce and hard—except for one. You rush up to him.

"Mercy!" you cry. "Spare my life!"

"Why should I spare your life?" he asks. "Are you my slave?"

"I am now." You are so scared that you do not even look up into his face.

"You agree to be my slave for the rest of your life?" he asks.

"I do," you say.

There is a long pause before he says, "Very well. It looks as if we'll make camp here until the dust storm moves on." You begin to help him set up camp as if your life depends on pleasing him, which it probably does.

That evening after you have fed your master his meal, your stomach is still growling for food. You notice that the cloud is dark on the Egyptian side. You wonder if it is light on the other side for the Israelites, as usual. The pillar of cloud changes to a pillar of fire every night for Israel. That way, the people always know God is with them.

You sigh. That night you go to sleep only after your master has. You sleep at his feet. The next morning, it is barely light when you hear shouts from others in the camp.

"The storm is lifting!"

You quickly help your master dress and pack his things. Within minutes he is in his chariot. You look toward where the cloud lifted, but the Israelites are not there.

Where did they go? you wonder.

"They'll not get away from us so easily," your master says. What could he mean? You look again. That is when you notice that the Red Sea has a path through it. God made a path through the Red Sea! All of your family and friends have crossed through the water on dry land. Amazing! Most of them are already across. The last of them are clear on the other side of the seabed, going up its banks. They look like ants, they are so far away.

Pharaoh's army gets into formation. The horses are ready for swift pursuit.

CHOICE ONE: If you move to the back of the army where the other servants and slaves are, go to page 48.

CHOICE TWO: If you jump on the back of your master's chariot, go to page 27.

You decide to keep going in the direction that you are already traveling. You are hoping that at some point, you will find a place to cross. Then you can travel back to meet up with your family. That is your goal anyway. When you finally reach a small village, you intend to stay there only a few days.

One of the farmers in the area takes a liking to you. "Why not stay here with us?" he says. You see that he needs help with his house, so you make bricks for him like you used to for the Egyptians.

When the people in the village realize that you know how to make the best bricks they have ever seen, they beg, "Do not leave us. You can make a good living for yourself here."

You think about their offer. "I'll stay for a while, but someday I must leave and find my family."

Life is relaxing in this village, and you like being paid for your work. You enjoy being treated like an adult, too. You like being known as the best brick maker in town. Later, you marry and have children of your own. As you grow older, you tell others of what you saw at the Red Sea. Everyone hears how powerful the God of Israel is.

THE END

You pick up food until your basket is full and set it by your bed. All day you snack on it. You cannot remember ever having so much food all to yourself. At night, you still have half a basket left. You do not want your mother to see it, and you do not want to have to share it with the twins, so you hide it under your blanket.

That night, you dream of eating sweet wafers under golden sunshine. At dawn, you are suddenly wide awake. A horrible smell makes you want to choke. Something is crawling on you. In fact, things are squirming all over you! You hop up and run out of the tent.

"What are you doing?" your father asks. You dance around trying to shake the bugs off. Your father follows you out into the morning light. "They're wormy maggots," he says.

"Oh no!" you exclaim. "Where did they come from?" You pick one out from between your toes.

Your father helps you brush them off. You go back into the tent. Your father holds the tent flap up to give you light. Maggots are all over your covers and mat.

"Where did they come from?" you ask.

"You didn't do what you were told." Your father points to your manna. Instead of wafers of bread, you have a basket crawling with maggots.

"I'm going to be sick." You run outside to throw up. After you clean yourself off, your father helps you shake your mat and covers. You clean the basket together, and then he makes you clean out the whole tent.

"God provided the manna for us to eat," your father says. "He told us not to save it, except on the Sabbath." His face gets stern. "Let's try trusting God and doing it His way from now on, okay?"

"Okay," you say.

From that day on, you only gather what you can eat in one day. Sometimes you even go a little hungry. The sight of manna almost makes you sick. You keep remembering that rotten smell and feeling the maggots crawling all over you. Manna never tastes quite as good to you again.

THE END

◆ ◆ ◆

You ignore what Esau is saying. What you experienced today is too wonderful. You will not let him spoil it. Several days later, you are at a place called Marah, where God does another miracle for you.

Moses tells all the Israelites to listen carefully to what the Lord tells them. He says to do what is right and to follow all God's commands. If you do, then God will protect you from the diseases that He brought on the Egyptians.

"For I am the Lord, who heals you," God says.

You believe it. Even though your feet are blistered and your face and hands are a little sunburned, you know that the Lord will keep His promise. He opened the Red Sea, didn't He? A God like that must really love you. You know that He can do anything!

THE END

◆　◆　◆

You decide to throw yourself on Pharaoh's mercy. Hopefully, he is feeling kind today. The dust cloud in the distance draws closer to you. It is enormous.

I know, you tell yourself, *maybe one of Pharaoh's soldiers will take me as his slave! Then I can beg for my family's lives too.* You hate the thought of being a slave again, but at least you will be alive. The idea makes more and more sense to you.

You hurry past the tents of the other Israelites and through the herds of goats in your way. The coast is clear. A twinge of fear runs down your back, and you hesitate. You look back in the direction of the camp. You love your family too much to let them die. If you can reach the Egyptians in time, you will beg for their lives and for your own.

You race toward the approaching Egyptian army. Suddenly, you realize that they are coming faster than you thought. What if they are moving too fast to see you?

CHOICE ONE: If you turn back, go to page 30.

CHOICE TWO: If you try to signal to them, go to page 41.

◆ ◆ ◆

You shrug.

"Come down and join us," Esau says.

You want to be with your friends, but what they are doing is wrong. Inside, you wrestle with what to say next.

Esau continues, "Quit scowling and smile. Life's about having fun."

"No, Esau, it's not." You stand up.

"Don't tell me you're a Moses follower." Esau rolls his eyes.

"I'm a follower of God," you say. "If He wants me to follow Moses, then that's what I'll do. What you're doing is wrong. I'm going."

A strange expression rests on Esau's face and the faces of the two friends next to him. They look uncomfortable.

One of them, Simeon, says, "I think I'll come with you."

As you leave, Esau taunts, "Moses lovers. Moses lovers."

From then on, you and Simeon spend a lot of time together and become good friends. Forty years later, Simeon thanks you. "If you hadn't stood up for what was right when you did, I would have died with Esau instead of entering the Promised Land."

Joyfully, you cross the Jordan River together.

THE END

◆ ◆ ◆

"Help! Help! We're going to die!" you scream. You and the twins run around in circles waving your hands in the air and kicking the sand. Suddenly, you run into one another, cracking heads. Pain shoots through your forehead. When you touch it, you feel a large gash. Your hand is covered with blood. You faint at the sight of it.

For a long time, you feel hot and far away. Every now and then you hear yourself cry out, "We're going to die!" When you finally wake, three days have passed. Everyone is safe. Was it all a dream? Did Pharaoh's army really come after you?

Mary and Mariah tell you an incredible story about walking on the bottom of the sea. They tend to exaggerate, so you don't believe them. Then your parents and friends tell the same story. Is this a joke? Are they trying to drive you crazy? Or did you sleep through the most awesome experience of your life?

You don't believe anyone until more miracles happen. Like when water comes from a rock and food falls from the sky. Then you're sorry you missed seeing the waters of the Red Sea part.

From now on, you're going to steer clear of Mary's and Mariah's heads.

THE END

Trapped!

Trapped!

"Talmai, let's spy!" you say. Spying is your favorite game.

Your brother scowls and says, "I can't. I've got to watch Onan." You wrinkle your nose. Your two-year-old brother does not make a good spy, and he smells like he needs to be changed. You hurry away before Talmai asks for your help.

Once out of sight of your home, you saunter along the streets of Jericho. The sun is painting long shadows across the city.

You turn down a path that runs between Jericho's wall and the almost empty marketplace. You hear two men approaching. Undetected, you slip between cool stones into your favorite hiding place in the city wall.

"Israelite spies here? In Jericho? Are you sure?" The voice is rough. The men walk along the street near where you are hiding. They are too close for you to peek out and identify them.

"I saw them myself," the other man says.

A shiver of fear creeps up your back. Real spies! You have heard that some strange, powerful people called Israelites are camped on the other side of the Jordan River. They have already defeated two mighty Amorite kings.

The men continue speaking as they move away from your hiding place. "Do you really believe that their God opened the Red Sea for them and then drowned the whole Egyptian army?"

The second man answers, "Yes, I do. Thousands of slaves couldn't possibly have defeated Pharaoh's chariots and horses. I just hope they're not planning to attack us."

"Jericho has a strong wall," says the first man. "If they dare attack, we can defeat them."

"But can we defeat their God?" asks the first.

You can no longer hear what the men are saying. You want to see the spies for yourself. You climb to a nearby roof to survey the area. You do not see anything out of the ordinary. The hay on the roof makes you sneeze.

Two men in dark robes hurry around the corner. The spies! Others are watching them like you are, only they are being more obvious. The men enter a house built into the city's wall.

Oh no! It's your Aunt Rahab's house! Aunt Rahab is your mother's sister. You like her, but she has a way of getting into trouble. You hope that the men won't hurt her. You wonder if she could get arrested for letting foreign spies into her home.

CHOICE ONE: If you go home for supper and tell your family what you saw, go to page 90.

CHOICE TWO: If you decide to visit Aunt Rahab to find out what is going on, go to page 92.

You are hungry, and supper should be ready. So you head for home. You enter the house and shut the wooden door behind you. The scents of freshly roasted lamb and vegetables fill the room. Talmai is playing on the floor with Onan. Your baby brother looks tiny beside Talmai, who is almost as tall as your father.

"I know something you don't," you whisper to Talmai.

He ignores you. He's probably still upset that you went spying without him. Onan giggles when Talmai tickles him.

"I only hope Aunt Rahab knows what she's doing." That ought to catch his interest. You start setting your family's clay dishes on the wooden table.

Talmai says, "Come here, Onan, and I'll tickle you again."

"It's too bad," you whisper, as if talking to yourself, "but if she has to die, I hope she leaves me her house."

Talmai stops and slams his hand on the floor. "What are you talking about?"

You can't help gloating a little. "I saw some real spies today. They're from the Israelite camp by the Jordan."

Talmai says, "You watch Onan. I want to go and see the spies."

Your mother walks in with a pitcher of goat's milk. "Help me put the food on the table, you two."

Talmai blurts out, "Aunt Rahab is in trouble, and there are spies in Jericho. Please, Mom. Let me go."

Your mother is used to you and your brother pretending to be spies. Her voice does not change. "Maybe later. I need your help now."

Talmai complains but obeys. You go to help your mother too.

During supper, your parents do not allow Talmai and you to tell spy stories, so Talmai tries to mouth questions to you. You don't understand him.

Talmai becomes frustrated and says, "I'm not going to wait until I grow up to be a soldier. I'll fight for Jericho against the Israelites now."

"I'm sure you will," your father says. "But don't talk with your mouth full."

You take a large bite of lamb to keep from laughing.

CHOICE ONE: If you describe the men to your brother after supper, go to page 163.

CHOICE TWO: If you continue teasing your brother after supper, go to page 106.

◆ ◆ ◆

You watch Aunt Rahab's house for a while, but the men do not come out. Finally, you climb down from your hiding place and go to Aunt Rahab's door. You stare at it. Should you knock? What if the men have killed her? What will they do to you? You start to turn away, but then you change your mind. You close your eyes, grit your teeth, and knock.

Aunt Rahab calls out, "Who is it?"

"It's me, Aunt Rahab," you shout.

After a few moments, the door opens. Your aunt greets you with a smile, but before she can hug you, a soldier rushes up.

"We've heard reports of Israelite spies here," he says. You can tell that he came from the king because of his uniform.

"We'd like to take a look around," says another soldier.

Aunt Rahab lets them in immediately. "There were some men here earlier," she tells them. "Were they really spies? I could have been killed! Oh, I'm so glad they left!"

You never saw the men leave. What is Aunt Rahab up to? Her house has only one door, and you were watching it the whole time. Your aunt is lying.

CHOICE ONE: If you do not say anything and wait for the soldiers to leave, go to page 141.

CHOICE TWO: If you tell the soldiers what you saw, go to page 113.

The moment your aunt is gone, you put Onan on the floor and ask, "Can I stay with Aunt Rahab?"

"Don't be ridiculous!" your mother says. Talmai laughs at you, but you believe that what Aunt Rahab says is true. You hear a clank and spin around. It's only Onan hitting his rocks together.

That night you have a hard time sleeping. You hear every creak of your house. During breakfast the next morning, you go to the window three times, thinking you have heard something.

"Why are you so jumpy?" your father asks.

"Israel's going to attack, and if we're not at Aunt Rahab's house, we'll die," you say.

"You don't think I can protect you from them?" your father asks.

"From them, maybe," you say, "but not from their God. May I please stay with Aunt Rahab?" Your father grunts and leaves the table.

For days you startle at every noise. You are so nervous that your parents become jumpy just being around you.

One day your mother says, "Oh, let the child go." Your father rolls his eyes, but he does not stop you.

Once inside Aunt Rahab's house, you finally feel safe. Her rooms are filled with beautiful fabrics, and she smells like a wildflower. You never want to leave Aunt Rahab's house again, not even to fetch water. Talmai visits to taunt you about being such a coward.

"If Israel attacks," he says, "I'll be a brave lion, not a scared rabbit like you. Our parents are ashamed of you, and so am I." His words hurt you inside.

"Talmai, that is enough," Aunt Rahab says. "An attack is coming, and you will die if you are not with me. Every day I visit your parents and try to convince them to stay with me, but they won't listen," she says.

If only you could think of a way to convince your family to come and be safe at Aunt Rahab's.

CHOICE ONE: If you never leave Aunt Rahab's house,
go to page 149.

CHOICE TWO: If you head home to try to convince
your family to stay at Aunt Rahab's house,
go to page 127.

"I don't know," you say, "but I want to get as far away from it as I can."

"No one is safe from magic like that," Talmai says.

"Aunt Rahab says it's their God. Let's leave now or their God might do something terrible to us for spying on them."

"We'd better go tell Mom and Dad," Talmai says. He rubs a dirty hand over his forehead as though he has a headache.

Your head hurts too. "That's the last thing we should do," you say. "If the Israelite God is after us, we'll put our family in danger by going home."

You both start running in the opposite direction of Jericho. You eat wild berries and roots whenever you can find them and drink from streams along the way.

When you finally reach a city, the people there seem just as afraid of Israel as Talmai and you are. You wonder if you can be safe there. Should you have listened to Aunt Rahab? Talmai and you find work carrying water and supplies in the local market for several weeks.

One night, Talmai says, "I want to go home. I miss Mom and Dad."

"And Onan," you add. You both think for a while before you continue. "Israel's God hasn't done anything to us yet. Perhaps it would be okay to go home," you say. You and your brother immediately begin the journey back to Jericho.

When you reach a hill overlooking Jericho, you see only a pile of blackened rubble. You race to where the city should have been, but it isn't there. Only one small section of the city wall seems undamaged.

Talmai and you begin to climb over ruins and dead bodies; the smell of decay and ashes is everywhere. You hold your noses and try not to look.

You reach the only house that is still standing.

The door has been burnt off and the inside has been gutted by fire. Sunlight is shining through the window, and you see something hanging outside. It has been singed, but you recognize it as Aunt Rahab's red cord.

"This is Aunt Rahab's house!" you shout. "See the cord?"

Talmai nods and then shakes his head. "I wonder if she made it out of Jericho okay."

"I wonder if our family was with her," you say.

You leave Jericho because there is nothing left for you there. You do not even look back. It is too painful.

"Aunt Rahab must be with the Israelites," you say. "Maybe if we go to them they will have mercy on us and let us stay with her."

"Aren't you afraid of what their God will do to us?" Talmai asks.

"I am more afraid of never knowing the truth. I want to find out if Aunt Rahab and maybe even our parents and Onan are alive." You head in the direction of the Israelite camp.

When you reach it, you are overjoyed to see your aunt alive. You and Talmai give her an enormous hug, but neither one of you can ask the question on your mind.

"I know it's only been a couple of weeks, but I think you've both grown," she says. Her eyes are moist as if she is about to cry, but she blinks the tears back. "Where have you been?"

You and Talmai tell her of your adventures. Then you stop and look to the ground. You are so afraid of finding out that your family did not survive.

Finally, Talmai asks, "Are our parents and Onan here?"

Aunt Rahab bites her bottom lip, and then says, "When you two disappeared, your father searched everywhere for you. He was a broken man. He was so distressed that he began to listen to what I said about Israel's God. He even got your mother to listen. When Israel attacked, your whole family was in my house. They are all safe."

You smile. Your heart feels light. Just then, you see your father in the distance. He's holding Onan. You and Talmai run to him and are engulfed in an enormous bear hug. If your father has chosen to believe in Israel's God, then you are going to believe in Him also.

THE END

You believe the rumors. Israel has been marching around the city one time each day for about a week. They are marching longer than normal this morning. Something must be up. Talmai and your father prepare to fight. You, your mother, and Onan run to your safest hiding place in Jericho's wall. You have put blankets, food, water, and extra clothing there. Now all you have to do is wait—and keep Onan quiet if the enemy gets near.

The sounds outside of your hiding place are dulled, because you are in the middle of the thickest part of the wall. Then you hear a sound as if the earth's stomach were growling. That sound is loud and is not muffled at all. Onan begins to cry. You feel like crying too. Your mother screams.

Without warning, Jericho's wall starts to shake. Your hiding place crumbles. The wall that you thought would protect you kills you and your family.

THE END

Since Onan likes going to the inn, and people from all over hang around it, you decide to go there. You stoop down to Onan's level and say, "Want to go to the inn? Want to see Father?"

Onan squeals with delight. He starts toddling toward the door. You pull him into your arms, laughing.

The streets are crowded with merchants selling their wares. Pigs, sheep, and goats wait in stalls for purchase, filling the air with grunting and bleating, as well as some odors you would rather not smell. You hurry past.

When you reach the inn, you set Onan in a chair with some dates to eat. He plays with them and gets his hands, face, and hair sticky.

While you are cleaning him, you hear a soldier say, "Israel has sent spies into Jericho."

"I heard that they escaped, so the king's men went after them," says a merchant.

"I hope you're right," says the soldier. "Those Israelites have some unbelievable power behind them."

A third man's voice cracks as he tells about the power of Israel's God. When you look up, you are surprised to see that most of the men look a little nervous. Some are even trembling! You catch your father's eye.

"Don't worry," your father says. "Jericho's wall will protect us."

"You aren't afraid then?" you ask. You move your weight from one foot to another.

"No, and you shouldn't be either. Now take this little boy home for his nap."

You wish you could be like your father. You know that Jericho's soldiers are strong and fierce. From the safety of your hiding places you have watched them fight. But you are afraid. You look at your little brother falling asleep sitting up. He is so cute. What if someone should hurt him?

CHOICE ONE: If you go home and talk to Talmai about what you heard, go to page 133.

CHOICE TWO: If you run away to protect your baby brother, go to page 109.

You leave for another city. The journey is long and hard. Onan sometimes walks and sometimes has to be carried. You do not know which is worse. When he walks, he stops to look at rocks, bugs, or plants every few feet. When you carry him, your arms and back ache.

After several days of walking, you have not come to a city. You should have been there by now. With a sinking heart, you realize that you are lost—and you have run out of food. You sit down and cry. Onan climbs on your lap, pats your face, and tries to make you feel better. You hug him.

"You feel better now?" he asks.

You do not want to disappoint him, so you say, "Yes, I feel better."

He hops off your lap. "Okay, we go play."

Moping around will not help, so you get up and chase Onan around some bushes. His giggles make everything seem okay again. You grab him and spin him around. "I love you, Onan," you say.

"I wuv you, too," he shouts between giggles. You set him down on the ground and support him while he regains his balance.

"I'm hungry," he says. Suddenly he points and squeals. "Horses!" Onan loves animals, but he sometimes gets mixed up on their names. You look behind you to see what's really there. Camels! It appears to be a caravan, and they are coming right toward you.

Could they be friendly? Surely they would not hurt two lost and starving children. You walk toward them. When you meet, the leader greets you. You tell him that you are lost. They are from a far-off country, and they offer to take you home with them.

"Are there any Israelites in your country?" you ask.

"What is an Israelite?" the leader asks.

"It doesn't matter," you say with a smile. You do not like leaving your home, but at least with this man you believe you and Onan will be safe. You offer yourself as his servant if he will help you take care of your brother.

You go to the man's home and serve his kind family for many years.

THE END

You start yelling and waving your arms, trying to convince your parents to go to Aunt Rahab's house. Talmai joins in.

"It's true! Every word. If you don't believe us and go to Aunt Rahab's house, we're all going to die!"

Your mother feels your foreheads. "You've both had too much sun today. Here, drink some water, and then I want you both to lie down."

"They're acting crazy," says your father as he leaves the room.

Finally, after days of pleading, they allow you both to go stay with Aunt Rahab. Your aunt is certain the attack will come soon. From her window in the city wall, you watch the forces of Israel march around the city, but afterwards they leave. You watch the army repeat this day after day. Talmai and you play games on the floor or help Aunt Rahab feed your relatives. Many have come to her house for safety. Talmai and you are worried about little Onan and your parents, who have not come. Finally, you work together to devise a plan.

After everyone is asleep, Talmai and you sneak out into the street. Silently, you work your way across town to your house. You climb through a window. Baby Onan is asleep on a mat. Talmai wraps him in a blanket and carries him to the window while you leave a note for your parents to come to Aunt Rahab's house. You are glad that your father taught you to write.

Your note says, "Onan is with us. Please come to Aunt Rahab's so we will all be safe together."

You climb out the window, and Talmai hands Onan to you. He stirs a little, but you rock him in your arms to get him back to sleep.

He feels much heavier when he's asleep. You take turns carrying him to Aunt Rahab's house.

In the morning, your parents come to Aunt Rahab's, but only to get Onan. They have no intention of staying.

"The least you can do is look out the window at the Israelites," Rahab says to try to convince them to stay. Out of curiosity, they do look out the window to see the soldiers, and they accept some of the food that Aunt Rahab has prepared with your help.

Finally, they get up to leave. Talmai and you have already planned for this. While they were not looking, you slowly piled rocks, furniture, bedding, and even some flax stalks from the roof against the door. You sit on top of them and refuse to move.

Your father is angry. Just as he is about to thrash you for your stubbornness, you hear a piercing note from the trumpets and loud shouting. You feel the earth shaking around you. The wall of Jericho has fallen, but the section at Aunt Rahab's house is still standing. Your family is safe!

THE END

◆ ◆ ◆

After dinner, Talmai and you go outside.

Talmai asks, "Who are these spies? What do they look like? Is Jericho in danger?"

"Could be. But I'd give up the idea of fighting back. The Israelite army is too strong."

"What are you talking about?"

You lean over the wall of the well and smell the moist stones. "Wouldn't you like to know!" You hurry past him toward your father's inn. Talmai follows.

He grabs your arm. "Tell me what's going on!"

You kick him to try to get away. Even though you pull and twist, he does not let go. Your hand is going numb. Just as you are about to give up and tell him what he wants to know, you see your father. You let out your most painful-sounding moan.

Just as you hoped, your father comes over and pulls you apart.

"Stop it, both of you!" He is about to leave.

Talmai's eyes narrow. You have pushed him too far. You do not want to be alone with him. You begin to wail.

"That's enough!" your father says. "Go home. Go to bed at once. Both of you. And I don't want to hear another sound from either of you!"

You run home before Talmai can take out his anger on you. You lie down on your mat and turn your face to the wall. Talmai arrives after you. Without a word, he moves his mat away from yours and falls heavily onto it. The room grows dark.

You begin to regret picking a fight with your brother. You try to whisper to him, but he has either fallen asleep or is refusing to talk to you. You decide to make it up to him in the morning by telling him everything.

When the sun rises, Talmai is gone, and so is your father's sword. You never see him again.

One day, you hear a rumor that he was killed trying to fight the Israelites all alone. You blame yourself. You are so upset that you ignore everything happening around you. Even the lamb that you normally love so well tastes bland.

Each day is a blur to you, until the day Israel attacks. The wall falls with a crash, and there is a cloud of dust in the air that makes it hard to breathe. You see a soldier coming at you with a sword. It is then that you come alive again. You want to avenge your brother's death. You grab a knife and a sharp stick and go toward him. You fight bravely, but you are no match for a grown-up warrior. You die in battle.

THE END

You hold still until the men disappear into the blackness of the Jericho plain. Just then, a guard comes by on his nightly rounds.

"You there!" You can see by the shadow of his bow and arrow that he is ready to shoot.

"Don't shoot! I'm a child of Jericho," you shout.

He lowers the bow and walks over to you. "Don't you know better than to play up here after dark?" he says. "I could have mistaken you for a spy. Now go home."

The soldier means business. You climb down as fast as you can.

"Don't let me catch you up here after dark again," he says.

You reach the street, panting. That was close.

CHOICE ONE: If you go to Aunt Rahab's to ask her about the strangers, go to page 135.

CHOICE TWO: If you go home and tell your brother what you saw, go to page 126.

You decide to try to protect your baby brother by running away. While he is taking his nap at home, you gather up food, clothing, and other supplies. You leave a note for your family and then sneak out, carrying the sleeping Onan.

When you reach the city gate, it is crowded with people. The adults are so busy arguing about Israel that no one notices you leaving. You make your way across the plain and hide in the hills nearby. One time you think you see two men who look like foreigners, but they quickly disappear. Could they be the spies who visited Aunt Rahab? If they are, then the king's men were looking for them in the wrong direction!

You play with your brother by day and sleep beside him at night. You have found a cave for your home. Each day, you go to a place where you can see Jericho and watch what is happening. It is strange, but no one seems to be coming or going. The gate never opens.

One day you see people marching from the plain to Jericho. It must be the Israelites! They are blowing horns of some kind. You can hear them faintly, but you can't quite see them. The army marches all the way around the wall that surrounds Jericho. Then they leave. You wonder what they are doing.

For the next three days, the same thing happens. You are not sure what to do, but watching Onan in the hills is getting harder and harder. Yesterday he was almost bitten by a snake, and you are beginning to run out of food. As you chew on a hard piece of bread that tastes more like your sandals than your mother's cooking, you decide to go home. The Israelites are probably not as bad as you imagined.

You wait until Onan is asleep. Then you pick him up and make your way back to Jericho's gate. It is locked! Try as you might, you can't get in. You have to go somewhere else, but where?

CHOICE ONE: If you leave for another city,
go to page 102.

CHOICE TWO: If you go back to the hills and wait for
the gate to open, go to page 142.

"Talmai sleeping?" Onan asks.

You shake Talmai, but he is still unconscious. "Come on, wake up," you say. "Onan, help me wake up Talmai."

Onan climbs on top of Talmai's stomach repeating, "Wake up! Wake up!" He tries to stand up and then plops his whole weight on Talmai's stomach.

Talmai groans. You help him sit up. His head is bleeding a little.

"Come on," you say to Talmai. "We have to get someone to fix that cut. Aunt Rahab's house is closest."

Talmai is too dazed to argue. You support him with one arm and carry Onan with the other. You feel as though your arms are breaking by the time you reach Aunt Rahab's house. She was watching for you.

"Quick," she says, "get inside." There is blood everywhere, and Talmai looks really pale. It scares you a little.

"Shouldn't we bring Mother and Father here to see to Talmai?" you ask as one of your other aunts cleans the wound.

Aunt Rahab opens her door and calls to a merchant across the street. "Abi, could your servant run and find my sister right away? Her son has been hurt. He's bleeding."

"Of course," Abi calls back.

"Please hurry! Please," Aunt Rahab says. The urgency in her voice makes you wonder. Talmai is hurt, but his wound is not life threatening. Could her urgency have something to do with the Israelites marching outside the city?

You want to look out the window, but you will not leave Talmai's side. You feel responsible for his injury, and you want him to know how sorry you are. Most of the family are crowded at the window, leaning out to see what is happening below.

Your cousin says, "This is the fourth time they are marching around." By the time your parents come through the door, your cousin says, "That makes the seventh time."

"Talmai, are you okay?" your mother asks. A loud shout from outside drowns her next words.

Almost immediately, there is a creaking and groaning, as if the very earth beneath you is moving. It becomes a rumble, like a thunderstorm, that shakes the house. Talmai holds on to you and your mother. Your father picks up Onan, and you huddle together. Everything shakes. A clay pot falls off one of Aunt Rahab's shelves and crashes to the floor. The room fills with a cloud of dust and covers each of you. It makes your eyes water and tastes like dry mud pies. Onan begins to cry, choking on the air as he gasps for breath.

You focus your eyes on the red cord hanging from the window, the sign to the Israelites that Aunt Rahab's family is inside. You hear yelling men and the screams of women along with the clanking of metal. Then suddenly Aunt Rahab's door bursts open, and Israelite soldiers stand in the doorway. Their faces are fierce looking and their weapons have blood on them.

"Rahab?" says the soldier in front. His voice is not as rough as he looks.

Aunt Rahab nods. "I am Rahab. These are my relatives."

"Come with me," he says, "all of you. We'll get you out of here safely." You give a sigh of relief. You did not know that you had been holding your breath. You are alive! Your whole family is safe!

From deep inside your heart, you give thanks to Israel's God. When you get out of here, you want to learn more about Him.

THE END

Aunt Rahab's lie could be putting the whole city in danger. "I saw the men, too," you say. "And they never—"

"Silence!" demands one of the soldiers. He pushes you aside. "We didn't ask you."

Aunt Rahab continues her story. "The men left at dusk, when the city gates were closing. If you hurry, you may be able to catch them." The men thank her and leave. "Go quickly!" she calls after them.

When the door is shut behind them, you look at your aunt suspiciously.

She smiles. "Sit down, dear. I have something to tell you."

You look around the room, wondering where the spies are hiding.

Aunt Rahab says, "Jericho is in great danger. Even if we fight against Israel, we will not win."

Her words frighten you. You look at the door, wanting to run out of it.

CHOICE ONE: If you stay and ask your aunt to explain, go to page 158.

CHOICE TWO: If you run out of the house, refusing to hear any more, go to page 129.

You carry Onan to Aunt Rahab's house and knock. She does not answer the door. She must not be home. You wander around the city for a while and show Onan the market stalls on the way home. The merchants are selling everything you can imagine—silk, salt, and fruits that do not grow around Jericho. You wonder if someday you would like to be a merchant.

When you arrive home, you find that Aunt Rahab is there, with your mother. They are yelling at each other.

Your mother says, "I refuse to listen to any more of your nonsense."

You lay Onan down for his nap. Then Talmai and you go outside. "What's going on in there?" you ask.

"Aunt Rahab wants us all to stay with her if Israel attacks. She says that that's the only way we'll be safe. Mother thinks she's crazy."

"What do you think?"

"I'm not sure. Some of what Aunt Rahab says makes sense. I want to find out more about it."

Aunt Rahab comes out. "Please, children. Come to my house when Israel attacks and try to get your mother and father there too." She leaves.

Later, you ask your mother, "What were you fighting with Aunt Rahab about? Was she being mean to you?"

Your mother laughs, but her face is angry. "She wasn't being mean to me but to all of Jericho. She helped Israelite spies!"

You shake your head. "Israel is our enemy." Still, you do not like it when your mother and Aunt Rahab are upset with each other.

Soon the gates of Jericho are closed, and no one is allowed in or out. You feel trapped. Now only soldiers are allowed on the top of the wall. That is where all your favorite spying spots are. Aunt Rahab's window provides a great view of the outside. But you do not want your mother to feel that you are siding with Aunt Rahab against her.

CHOICE ONE: If you stay away from Aunt Rahab's house, go to page 137.

CHOICE TWO: If you visit Aunt Rahab, go to page 154.

◆ ◆ ◆

You shake your head. "She let foreign spies enter her home. How can we believe what she says?"

Talmai adds, "Maybe she even helped them to escape."

The thought that Aunt Rahab might have helped Jericho's enemy eats away at you for days. When you can't take it anymore, you ask Talmai, "Do you want to sneak out of Jericho with me and spy on the foreigners?"

"We'll leave as soon as the gates open tomorrow," Talmai says.

The next morning, the weather is perfect for spying. You pass through the city gate as if you have no more on your mind than catching dinner.

"Hello," you call to the two gatekeepers. "It looks like good weather for fishing at the Jordan River today."

"Watch out for foreigners," one of them warns.

"We will." You wave to thank him for his advice and move on. Your heart is beating violently with excitement, so you make yourself take deep, slow breaths.

Finally, you and Talmai are out of the city. You love the smell of the wild grasses around Jericho. You break off an especially long weed and stick it between your teeth.

"I'll race you to the river," Talmai says, hitting the end of the weed and sprinting away from you.

It is too far to run the entire way. When you both get tired, you walk side by side. By midmorning you have found the area across the river from where the Israelites are camping. Talmai finds a great hiding place behind some bushes. You join him. The Israelites appear to be packing up.

"Maybe they're going back the way they came," you say. "They certainly can't get all those people and supplies across the river. Look how the water is swelling. It's practically ready to flood over the banks."

As if on cue, the wind changes and blows wildly in your direction. The roar of the water almost drowns out Talmai's voice. "What do you think that box is? Do you see it?"

You scan the opposite bank. At first, you see only hundreds of people milling around. Then you notice some men carrying a large box on poles. It looks like it is made out of gold with wings on the top of it. It takes four men in fancy clothes to carry it. The men walk as if they are performing some type of ritual. They slowly make their way to the river. Suddenly, a deafening roar and a strong wind make both Talmai and you close your eyes and duck.

"Aaaahhh!" Talmai and you scream.

By the time you look up, you can't speak. The river upstream has stopped flowing.

Downstream, the water has all run off. There is no river at all!

The robed men have carried the strange box with poles into the riverbed. You expect them to sink or at least slip on the muddy bottom, but they are walking on dry land! All the Israelite soldiers and their families start crossing the Jordan as if there had never been a river there.

"Let's get out of here!" Talmai says.

You both take off running. Talmai is ahead of you. As you try to catch up, your heart is beating so hard that you can hardly breathe. You run until you can no longer see where the river used to be. Finally, you both stop to rest.

"What was that box?" Talmai asks. "What kind of magic did they use?" The heat from the sun is beating down on you, but you are shivering with fear.

You try to answer between pants. "I don't know. But now I'm sure that Aunt Rahab was telling the truth." Your side aches.

"What should we do?" Talmai asks.

CHOICE ONE: If you run as far away as you can, go to page 95.

CHOICE TWO: If you go back to Jericho to warn your family, go to page 147.

Y ou move closer to the edge of the wall so you can see a little better. The man has reached the ground. Holding onto the wall, you lean over farther to see his face in the moonlight. A section of the wall comes loose, and your hand slips. You try to catch yourself, but you leaned over too far. As you tumble over the edge, you remember hearing that people see their whole life passing before their eyes before they die. Twelve years goes by really fast.

THE END

You ignore Talmai, pick up Onan, and run to Aunt Rahab's house. You are glad that Talmai does not follow you. Instead of playing, you sit and think. Today's incident with Talmai scared you. Your family is putting Onan's life at risk. Before your mother comes to take him home, you hide him in one of your secret hiding places in the wall. It's not far from Aunt Rahab's, so you can get him to safety quickly.

"I'll come back for you in just a little while," you tell him. He's sleepy, so you cover him with a blanket and give him a toy made of lamb's wool to hold. He falls asleep.

When your mother comes to get Onan, you tell her that he is hidden, and you will not tell anyone where he is unless the whole family comes to Aunt Rahab's.

"Israel has been marching around this city every day," you say. "One of these days, they're not just going to march. They're going to attack. I can't let Onan die." Your mother is upset and worried about Onan. Aunt Rahab and the other relatives finally convince her to come stay with you all.

"Anyway," Aunt Rahab says, "if they don't attack, what could it hurt? We'll just have a family reunion. If they do attack, then you will all be safe with us."

Your mother promises to come the next day. You assure her that Onan will be safe with you. As soon as she leaves, you go get your brother. He snuggles into your arms. You are grateful that your plan worked, and that he will be safe.

The next morning, Israel's soldiers change their routine. You feel sure the attack is coming. The rest of your family has not yet made it to Aunt Rahab's.

CHOICE ONE: If you wait at Aunt Rahab's for them to come, go to page 125.

CHOICE TWO: If you run home to get your family, go to page 156.

You calm down, take a deep breath, and tell your story again, including every detail you can remember. Your mother's eyes soften a little, but your father becomes stern.

"Enough of your spy stories," he tells you. "Get to your chores." Talmai and you go outside to thresh some barley.

As you beat the stalks to release the grains, Talmai asks, "Why won't they believe us?"

"If you think about it, why would they believe us? We watched something that should have been impossible. And we have told some whopping spy stories before."

"I guess you're right. All we can do is keep telling them the truth until they believe us."

You think Talmai's idea is a good one. Every day, you both tell your parents about your frightening experience at the Jordan River. Rumors that support your story are spreading around the city. Finally, your parents believe you.

Then one day, the Israelites show up outside the city wall. Immediately, your father sends you, your brothers, and your mother to Aunt Rahab's house.

"Aren't you coming?" you ask your father.

"I have to take care of the inn," he says.

At your aunt's house, Talmai and you watch the Israelites from the window in the wall. They do not try to attack. They do not even look like they want to attack. They just march around the city. Then they leave.

"What was that for?" Talmai asks.

You shrug. Soon you all head for home.

The next day, the same thing happens. And then again a third day and a fourth day. Tomorrow will be the fifth day. The Israelites must be planning to attack soon. Each morning, you have begged your father to come with you, but he says he needs to take care of his customers at the inn. Since your father will not listen to you, you decide to try a different tactic.

CHOICE ONE: If you go to the inn with your father, go to page 160.

CHOICE TWO: If you try to force him to go to Aunt Rahab's, go to page 145.

You wait for your family to come, just as your mother promised. Over and over, you watch out the window to see what Israel is doing and then run to the door to watch for your family. Finally, when Israel has almost marched around the city for the seventh time, your parents arrive.

"Where's Talmai?" you ask, with terror in your heart.

"He refused to come," says your mother. "Maybe he'll change his mind later."

But it is too late. The walls come crashing down around you. Only those in Aunt Rahab's house survive.

THE END

◆ ◆ ◆

You run home. After supper, you pull your brother Talmai aside and whisper, "Listen." You tell him about what you saw.

He says, "I've heard people talking today about Israel. They defeated two powerful Amorite kings on the other side of the Jordan River."

That scares you. "Do you think they'll come here?"

"Let them come," he says.

Talmai is bigger and stronger than you are. Perhaps it is easier to be brave when one is not so small. He continues, "They can't possibly get through our city wall, but if they do, we'll beat them. I'm ready to fight."

You nod, but you are still a little scared. The next day, it is your turn to watch Onan. You think about taking him either to the inn or to see Aunt Rahab. You want to talk to someone about what you saw or at least gather more information.

CHOICE ONE: If you go to the inn, go to page 100.

**CHOICE TWO: If you go see Aunt Rahab,
go to page 114.**

You have seen Israel's campsite out on the plains. You know they will attack soon. Your heart aches to think that harm will come to your family. Reminded of how much you love your family, you open the door, step outside, and walk away from Aunt Rahab's house.

When you reach home, your father says, "Who is this stranger?"

Your mother's hug is so tight and long that you wonder if she will ever let you go. You don't mind, really. You have missed her and the good smells of her cooking that are deep within everything. Even Talmai's punch on your arm and Onan's slobbering kiss welcome you.

"Please come back to Aunt Rahab's with me," you say. "Israel has crossed the Jordan and is camped just beyond Jericho."

Your father says, "Jericho's wall has been built and rebuilt over hundreds of years. It is so strong and thick that no army can breach it. Stop worrying so much and stay home."

"Yes, stay and help," says Talmai. "I'm sick of doing your chores and mine too."

His words give you an idea. "I'm going back to Aunt Rahab's, but I can take Onan with me. I can take care of him there. That will help, won't it?"

"That would lessen Talmai's load," your mother says. "You can come get Onan in the morning, and then I'll come to take him home each evening."

"I'll watch Onan," Talmai says. "Watching him is easy compared to the other chores." You wonder if big, strong Talmai really means that or if he's going to miss Onan.

You say, "Onan can stay with me day and night."

Your mother shakes her head. "During the day is enough."

"That's not fair." Talmai pouts when no one pays him any attention.

Next day, you carry Onan's things in a sack and take him to Aunt Rahab's house. He wants to get down and walk partway. You watch him toddle on his chubby legs, and you are glad that he will be at the house with you. Every few feet, he stops to pick up a stone or to peek through a doorway. It's funny how a simple walk can be such a great adventure to a two-year-old.

When you reach Aunt Rahab's house, you feel a little less afraid. Aunt Rahab is delighted to have Onan around. Each evening your mother comes to get him. Sometimes she stays to talk with her sister and the other relatives who are living there. Each morning, you run home to bring Onan back.

Whenever you do, Talmai says, "Don't take him. It's not fair the way you have split up our family. Onan is my brother too. I'll watch him." You are surprised at how soft your brother's heart has become.

One day, he follows after you, trying to get Onan back. You hear Israel's trumpets in the distance and know that they are already marching around the city. You have a feeling that the attack will come soon.

CHOICE ONE: If you pick up Onan and run to Aunt Rahab's house, go to page 121.

CHOICE TWO: If you try to convince Talmai to go with you, go to page 134.

The more you think about the spies, the more scared you become. "I have to go," you say.

"Wait," she pleads. You ignore her words and race down the darkening streets, weaving your way through empty market stalls. You are looking back when someone blocks your path. You practically bounce off his protruding belly.

"Uncle Bela!" You give him an enormous hug. Your father's brother is your favorite uncle. "I'm sorry I bumped into you. I didn't see you there." He is a traveling merchant and comes to Jericho only twice a year. "When did you get here?" you ask.

"Oh, I've been here a few days. Been meaning to get over to see your family. No time now, though."

"Why not?"

"I've been hearing rumors, and I don't like them one bit. Those Israelites—have you heard of them?"

"Yes, I think they sent some spies here."

"Well, that does it for me. I'm getting out of town tomorrow."

You do not know what makes you say it, but you ask, "Can I go with you? I want to get out of Jericho too."

Your uncle rubs his chin. He always does that when he is thinking. "Why not? In fact, I think your whole family should come with me. I've been meaning to talk to your father about a business idea. His inn is doing pretty well here, but I believe that he would do much better in my town. With my goods and his know-how, we could be a great success."

Your uncle goes home with you. He and your father talk well into the night. Finally, it is decided. You will all go with your uncle. You take all your possessions with you. It takes seven days to reach your uncle's town.

At first, the new city is strange to you. You learn to like it after being there only two full moons. Every day you help your father at his new inn. Travelers coming to the inn talk about all the cities Israel has defeated, including Jericho. When you overhear their conversations, you wonder what happened to Aunt Rahab. You hope your new city will not be the next to fall.

THE END

◆ ◆ ◆

When you really think about what your aunt said, it makes sense. Gods of wood and stone are not gods at all. You decide to trust Aunt Rahab.

On your way home, you round the corner where you first saw the strangers. Was it only a coincidence that you spotted them? Maybe there was a reason. Tomorrow you will try to find out more about the Israelites and their God.

The next day, you help your father at the inn. You listen carefully to what his customers are saying.

One man says, "The Israelite God has magical powers to open up the sea."

You ask your father, "What does that man mean?"

"It was years ago at the Red Sea," he says. "The Israelites used to be slaves in Egypt. Pharaoh's army was chasing after them, and supposedly the sea opened up for the Israelites. Then it closed in over Pharaoh's army. I'm not sure I believe it, though. Here, serve this at table six."

You take two earthenware platters of meat and vegetables to a table near the door.

One man is talking to his companions at the table. "I've never heard of a god who can open up seas and help a bunch of slaves defeat powerful armies."

"It's true," another says. "And they defeated not one, but two Amorite kings, Sihon and Og." By his dusty clothes you can tell he has been traveling.

"Two?" The man whistles. "They must have learned soldiering from the Egyptians."

"No, it's just this God of theirs. The power they have is like nothing I've ever seen before. How can we begin to fight such a force?"

"Maybe we can find their god and steal it from them. Then we could have the power."

"That's just it. No one has even seen their God. It's as though He's alive and invisible. This whole business scares me. I'm getting as far away from here as I can, and I'd advise you to do the same."

All the talk frightens you. When your father is looking the other way, you slip out and start running as fast as you can. When you stop for breath, you are near the city wall. If you turn to the right, the road will take you to Aunt Rahab's house. If you turn left, it will take you to the city gate.

CHOICE ONE: If you turn right, go to page 143.

CHOICE TWO: If you turn left, go to page 150.

◆ ◆ ◆

You go home, put Onan to bed with a kiss, and find Talmai. You tell him about what you heard.

"I'm scared of Israel's God," you say. You grab a fig from the table and pop the sweet, gritty fruit into your mouth. You chew it quickly.

Talmai waves a hand at you. "I don't know why you and Jericho's soldiers are scared. You're all a bunch of cowards!"

"But Talmai, men can't fight the gods," you say.

"I'm ashamed of you and them," he says. "Jericho needs soldiers who will stand up to their enemies without fear. I am not afraid to fight."

You feel ashamed for your cowardice. Talmai makes plans to practice with your father's sword every day. You decide to ignore your fears and do something about the upcoming battle. You search all of Jericho for the best hiding places. When the time comes, you will be able to keep Onan safe.

Aunt Rahab comes over to talk to your family about the spies. "Come to my house, please." Your father and brother leave the room, and your mother shakes her head no. Even you do not look her in the eyes.

Then one day, you hear rumors that Israel is going to attack.

CHOICE ONE: If you believe the rumors, go to page 99.

CHOICE TWO: If you don't believe the rumors, go to page 162.

◆ ◆ ◆

You turn to Talmai with Onan in your arms. "Why should Onan die because you are so stubborn? Jericho doesn't have a chance against Israel."

"How can you say that? All they do is march around. They're too scared even to attack." Talmai looms over you. You know that if he wanted to, he could force you to give up Onan.

"Israel does not seem to be the fierce army I expected," you admit. "But their God is strong. Aunt Rahab has told me that their God is the one we should fear." You lean against a building and feel the coolness of the stones on your back. From a nearby house, you smell the scent of someone cooking sweet berries, just as if it were a normal day.

"You're a traitor!" Talmai whispers. "You're a traitor to our city and our gods. What if the king hears you? His soldiers will kill you and Onan, too. I won't let you take him." He snatches Onan from you.

Before he can leave, you grab on to Talmai's arm and hold it with all your strength so that he cannot leave with Onan. Onan starts crying.

Talmai tries to comfort him. "It's okay, little one." His arms loosen. You see your chance. You grab Onan. Talmai staggers backward and falls with a thunk! His head hits a stone wall, and he lies there unconscious.

CHOICE ONE: If you take Onan safely to Aunt Rahab's and then return to help Talmai, go to page 139.

CHOICE TWO: If you try to wake up Talmai, go to page 111.

You give in to your curiosity and decide to go to Aunt Rahab's house. "It's me again, Aunt Rahab," you call as you knock. She lets you in immediately.

She seems happy to see you. "What brings you back so soon?"

You pull her away from the door, just in case someone passing by can hear you. "I was on top of the wall and saw the men climb down from your window. What's going on?"

"I couldn't say anything earlier, but they were Israelites."

"And you let them go? Why?" you ask.

Your aunt sits you down and pulls a chair close to yours. "I did it to save our family. Israel is going to defeat Jericho."

This statement makes you angry. You stand up and face her. One of her soft pillows falls to the floor.

"Jericho is strong!" you say. "Just look at the wall out there. Your own house is built on it."

Aunt Rahab rests her hands on your arms. "Listen to me," she says. "Every man in Jericho is trembling with fear because of these Israelites and their God."

"My father isn't afraid. He says it's all just a bunch of rumors and that our gods will protect us." You wish your father were here right now, holding his strong arms around you.

She holds your hands in hers. "What are Jericho's gods made of?"

You have to think about it before answering. "Stone, wood, and stuff like that."

"Where did they come from?"

"The carvers made them. You know that." You wonder where she is going with this conversation. Everyone in Jericho knows the old man who chips away at wood and his brother who carves stones into the shapes of the gods.

"So you believe that these gods carved by men and made of stone and wood can save you?" Aunt Rehab asks.

When you think of it that way, it does not make any sense.

She continues. "Israel's God is a living God, more powerful than we can imagine. I believe in their God." You should not have been surprised. Aunt Rahab has always been a little different.

Aunt Rahab continues. "The spies promised they would keep our family safe when their God gives Israel the land. But everyone has to be inside my house, or they will die."

You are not sure what to believe. Why should you or your aunt trust what the Israelites said? Were they just lying to save themselves? Or were they telling the truth?

CHOICE ONE: If you decide that your aunt was fooled
by the spies, go to page 151.

CHOICE TWO: If you decide to trust your aunt's
judgment, go to page 131.

You decide to stay away from Aunt Rahab's house to please your mother, but you are curious to find out more about the Israelite spies. Since Talmai runs errands for your father for the next few days, you ask him to visit Aunt Rahab and find out all he can. In that way, he can tell you what he finds out. You stay home and help your mother.

After a few days, you see a difference in Talmai. He does not seem as ready to fight as before.

"What would it hurt to go to her house?" he asks. "We can fight there just as easily as anywhere else. And if what Aunt Rahab says is true, then we'll be safe."

What Talmai says makes sense. You both start working on your parents to get them to agree to go to Aunt Rahab's house.

Your mother says, "I'll think about it." Your father will not even consider it.

One day when you are working outside and watching Onan, Talmai comes running. "Come quickly, before it's too late!"

"Is it the attack?" you ask.

"Yes, hurry!" he says. Both of your parents are at the inn. You hurry there and try to get them to come with you.

"You go ahead," your mother says. "I'll come a little later."

"An attack?" your father says sarcastically. "What a bunch of nonsense."

You, Talmai, and Onan are in Aunt Rahab's house when the wall falls down. After the attack, you are orphans. You and your brothers live with Aunt Rahab and the Israelites. Talmai is the first to believe in Israel's God. At first, you do not want to believe, because you are angry about your parents' deaths.

"They had a chance to be saved," Talmai reminds you. "It was their choice not to go to Aunt Rahab's house."

Finally, you believe in the living God, too, and Talmai and you talk to Onan about Him every day.

THE END

You take off your cloak and cover Talmai with it. Then you pick up Onan and race to Aunt Rahab's house.

You tell her, "Talmai tried to take Onan from me. Then he fell back and hurt his head." You give Onan a big hug and leave him with your aunt. Then you rush back to where you left Talmai. He is still unconscious.

You try shaking him as you call, "Talmai. Talmai! Talmai, wake up!" He still does not revive.

You roll him onto your cloak. His head is bleeding a little. You pull on the cloak to drag Talmai along the street. When you go over a big bump, Talmai wakes up.

"What happened?" he asks.

"You hit your head. It's bleeding, and we have to get someone to bandage it." You help him struggle to his feet.

Suddenly, he remembers. "Where's Onan? We've lost Onan!"

"Calm down," you say. "He's safe at Aunt Rahab's. You'll see him in a few minutes."

Talmai stands and takes a step. He is moving very slowly.

"I'm dizzy," he says. "I want to stop and rest, maybe take a nap in the shade."

"No!" you say. "You hit your head hard. You have to stay awake until Aunt Rahab looks at you."

Step by step, you get closer to her house. You can hear the trumpets and the marching outside the city, and your heart beats faster. You have to reach the door in time!

The sound of loud trumpets and many voices shouting jolts you, and Talmai looks at you with wide-eyed fear. "What was that?"

Before you can answer, the wall of the city begins falling. You dodge debris, still trying to get to Aunt Rahab's. Her door is in sight. You pull Talmai with you as you work your way in that direction. You hear something above you. Rocks from a crumbling house are falling toward your head!

Talmai pulls you aside. You tumble to the ground, but unbelievably, none of the rocks lands on you. But now you will have to climb a small mountain of rubble to get to Aunt Rahab's. You are shocked to realize how silent everything is. Then you hear shouts and screams. Israelite soldiers are attacking and killing anyone left alive. Aunt Rahab's door is only a few feet away. The soldiers are approaching. Can you make it?

"Aunt Rahab! Aunt Rahab!" you shout. The door flies open. Two of your uncles rush out and grab Talmai. You are almost to the door. You trip on loose stones, but your hand lands inside the doorway. Your father's strong arms pull you in and shut the door just in time. Your father, mother, Onan, Talmai, and you are in Aunt Rahab's house.

You give your parents a hug. You and your family are safe!

THE END

You decide not to say anything. You just listen. Aunt Rahab tells the soldiers, "Those men—the ones you say are from Israel—have already left the city. If you hurry, you can catch them."

When the soldiers are gone, Aunt Rahab turns to you. "I'm so happy to see you, dear! But would you mind coming back another time? I have something I need to do."

Your aunt is up to something! You leave, but you sneak up onto the city wall to spy on her house. You watch her door until the moon is bright. The breeze is getting chilly, and you are about to give up and go home when you hear movement on the outside of the wall. You rush over to the edge. A long rope is being let down from Aunt Rahab's window. A shadowy figure slides through her window and climbs down the rope to the ground. Another follows. The second person is halfway down the wall.

CHOICE ONE: If you hold still until the men are out of sight, go to page 108.

CHOICE TWO: If you try to get closer to see better, go to page 120.

◆ ◆ ◆

You return to the hills and wait for the city gates to open. Israel comes back and marches around the wall once every day. One day, they don't stop after the first time around. They keep marching. You try to count how many times they march around Jericho. Is it seven? Suddenly, the trumpets sound louder, and there is a roar of shouting people. All at once, the wall of the city collapses! The Israelites charge up and over the crumbled wall. You tremble as you watch your hometown being destroyed. Tears stream down your face. You hold tightly to your sleeping brother.

When you are about to give up hope, you notice that one part of the wall is still standing. Could it be near Aunt Rahab's? It seems to be in about the right place. A little while later, you see some people being led out of the city by Israelite soldiers. You could not mistake Uncle Izri's funny walk. It has to be your relatives! You hurry to catch up with them, straining to see if your parents and Talmai are with them.

You call, "Wait up," to some cousins at the back of the group. One of them stops the others. When you catch up, your mother is the first to greet you. She wraps you and Onan in her arms and weeps for joy.

"I thought I had lost you," she says. "I thank the God of Israel for saving you both!" The three of you are all that is left of your family.

THE END

You turn right. When you reach Aunt Rahab's house, you do not even stop to knock. You throw the door open and shut it fast behind you.

"What's wrong? You look like the king's army is after you," Aunt Rahab says.

You grab her. "It's Israel's God. You've got to save me. I don't want to die."

Aunt Rahab tries to calm you down. "You don't have to die, remember? I told you that if you are in my house when the battle comes, you will be saved. Haven't you heard about Israel's God and all He has done for Israel? He takes good care of His people."

"But why does He want to destroy Jericho?" you ask.

"I don't know," she says. "But this is an evil city, just like the Amorite cities. I believe that Israel's God is good. I am convinced that He is God in heaven and on earth. That's why I helped the spies when they came to me."

She stops and takes your face in her hands. She looks deeply into your eyes. "I believe that Israel's God is the only real God. He will save us—you, me, and our whole family." You see a look of peace in your aunt's eyes. Suddenly, you are not afraid anymore. She lets go.

Soon you are running again, but this time you are running home. You tell Talmai what Aunt Rahab said, and you keep mentioning it to your parents.

One day, you hear that Israel's army is approaching. The gates of Jericho are barred shut against them. Talmai and you run to one of your hiding places in the wall to watch. Just in case the attack is coming, you pick a place near Aunt Rahab's house.

At the front of the Israelite army, seven men blow trumpets that look like they're made of rams' horns. Armed soldiers follow. Then you see men carrying a large box on poles. Instead of trying to scale the wall or trying to ram down the gate, they just march in a line around the wall of Jericho. Then they leave.

Talmai and you look at each other and shrug. It is the same the next day. And the next. And the next. Their quiet routine scares you more than an outright attack. All the people of the city are getting jittery. They are like rats trapped in a cage. No one knows what Israel plans to do.

On the seventh day, you are expecting the same thing, but there's a change. You see the men with the trumpets starting around the wall for a second time. This must be the day!

"Come on!" you say, grabbing Talmai's hand. "We've got to go to Aunt Rahab's house now." You hope the rest of your family will come.

When you arrive, you say to your aunt, "Tell Talmai about Israel's powerful God." While she is explaining, the Israelites keep marching around Jericho. More and more of your relatives are piling into Aunt Rahab's small house. There is no sign of your parents and your little brother, Onan.

You go back to the window to see what is happening. The large box is passing under you. Suddenly, you feel the need to pray to this God of Israel. You ask Him to save your family.

Just as the men of Israel begin to give a loud shout, Aunt Rahab's door creaks open. Your parents walk through it. When your mother sets Onan down, he runs toward you and Talmai. You pick Onan up and hug him, giving thanks to Israel's God for saving your family.

THE END

On the fifth day, you try another tactic to get your father to stay at Aunt Rahab's house. You wake up early and gather your father's cloak, girdle, and sandals. His tunic will look funny without the girdle around his waist, and that will embarrass him. Besides, he needs the girdle to hold his knife and other tools. Talmai sees what you are doing, but he does not give you away. You sneak out of the house and go to Aunt Rahab's early.

Just as you planned, your father comes to Aunt Rahab's with your mother and brothers to retrieve his clothes.

"Since you're here," Aunt Rahab says, "you might as well break the fast with us." Your father stays to eat, but he leaves before the Israelites start marching around Jericho. You are disappointed that your tactic failed.

The next morning, you take your father's clothes and his money. Without his money, he can't give change to his customers. Again, he comes to Aunt Rahab's house to get his things.

"Please stay with us," you say.

"Not today," your father says with a grimace. He stays to eat the morning meal and talks for a while with other relatives. When the Israelites have marched halfway around the city, he leaves just in case he has customers.

On the seventh day, you take his clothes, his money, his knife, and his ledger. He can't possibly do business without those things. He comes to Aunt Rahab's and walks in laughing.

"You've convinced me. I'll stay. Business is bad anyway. The people seem to prefer watching the Israelites more than eating my food."

You all watch out the window. Today is different. Instead of going around once, the army marches around Jericho many times. Talmai counts seven. Suddenly, they all stop. The trumpets sound, clear and loud.

Then you hear a deafening roar of voices and rumblings as though the earth is quaking. You all huddle in the middle of the room. You close your eyes until the noise dies down. When you open them, you can see clouds of dust, but nothing in Aunt Rahab's house has been broken except a clay pot.

You hold your breath. The world seems to be moving fast and slowly at the same time. By the time the door opens and Israelite soldiers enter, you are not quite sure what is happening. The soldiers lead your family through Jericho. You see that the wall has fallen, and Israelite soldiers are killing everyone in the city.

You feel panicky until your father says to you, "You saved my life." Then slowly, your world rights itself. You and your family are safe. Your father slides his arm around your shoulders, and you leave Jericho together under the protection of Israel's God.

THE END

You feel like running as far away as you can, but you think of baby Onan and your parents. "Let's go back home and tell Mom and Dad what we saw," you say. "Maybe if we all go to Aunt Rahab's, Israel's God won't destroy us."

Talmai looks doubtful, but he is too scared to argue with you. You start for home.

When you arrive in Jericho, the city seems the same as when you left it. If only the people knew what you had just seen! You race home, but no one is there.

"Let's check the inn," Talmai says.

You find your parents there. Your mother is helping serve food to guests. The lamb-and-lentil dish that your mother is serving smells good. Your stomach growls. Onan is playing peacefully behind a chair.

"Where have you two been?" your mother asks. "I've been so worried about you!"

"To the Jordan River to see the Israelite camp," you say.

Talmai says, "They made the river stop! Just like that!" He claps his hands for emphasis. Everyone in the inn starts to chuckle. You can see that no one believes Talmai.

You rise to his defense. "It's true. We saw it! They carried a big gold box into the water and suddenly they were walking on dry ground. They didn't even get their feet muddy." This time, only a few laugh.

"Your children have had too much sun," one man says to your father. He slaps his hand on the table and stands up to leave. Others look at you strangely, as if they are wondering if your story could be true.

"Enough of this nonsense," your father says. You can tell he is embarrassed. "Take your baby brother home and get to your chores, both of you."

That evening you try again to convince your parents of what you saw. Talmai and you repeat your story. Your parents think it is just another of your wild, made-up spy tales.

Your father concludes, "This time you even scared yourself." He laughs. You feel your face turning red. What can you do to make your mother and him understand?

CHOICE ONE: If you calm yourself down and try to tell your story again, go to page 123.

CHOICE TWO: If you start yelling and waving your arms trying to convince them, go to page 104.

Each day, you ask Aunt Rahab, "Do you think my family will come today?" She shakes her head no. You look out her window, past the scarlet cord she has hung as a signal to Israel. Israel has crossed the Jordan River and is now camped on the plains.

You could go and beg your family to come to Aunt Rahab's, but what if Israel attacks while you are away? You might not be able to make it back in time. You can never quite bring yourself to leave the house. One day the door opens to reveal an older man.

"Grandfather!" you say and give him a big hug. Another day, the door opens and Uncle Ui is there with his wife and three daughters. Aunt Rahab's house is becoming crowded, but at least there are other children to play with.

Aunt Rahab feeds you well, but you miss the herbs that your mother used. The lamb your mother cooked seemed to melt in your mouth. Every day, a few more relatives join you at Aunt Rahab's. She has done a good job of convincing everyone—except your family.

When the attack comes, you are saved, along with many other relatives. You try not to think about your family. You know they are dead, but the thought hurts too much. For the rest of your life, you regret that you were not bold enough to leave Aunt Rahab's house to try to save your family.

THE END

◆ ◆ ◆

You turn left. The city gates loom up in front of you. They are open. You do not even stop to look back. You feel tingling on your spine as though someone or something is following you, so you run faster. Your mind dulls your senses in a nightmare of terror. You keep running. Finally, you reach a nearby city. You stay there a while, until you hear that Israel's army has defeated Jericho and is on the way.

Then you run again—to the next city, and the next, until finally you can run no more. Your muscles ache, but your mind aches more. You live in the open. No one gives you shelter. A fever makes your eyes hurt when you open them. You know you smell like vomit. You climb to the top of the wall that surrounds the city you now live in. You do not even remember its name. You stand up to breathe some fresh air. In the distance, you see a dust cloud.

"They're coming," someone shouts. "Israel is coming!"

People are screaming and crying all around you. Soldiers are getting ready to fight. You know it is no use. They can't hide from Israel's God. You tried, and it did not work. The thought comes to you that you should have believed Aunt Rahab. You lie back down on the cold stone and prepare to meet your doom.

THE END

You shake your head. "You're believing a lie, Aunt Rahab. They only told you that to make you do what they wanted you to do." With that, you leave.

The next morning, you go to report Aunt Rahab to the king's men. When you get to the palace, one of the guards is yelling at a dog to chase it away. The dog obviously wants food. It sits down in front of the man, turns its head sideways, and whines.

Finally, the guard kicks the poor dog and yells, "Get away from here!" It leaves.

You hesitate. What if the guard kicks you, too? You start to turn away and go home. Then you remember that your city is in danger because of your aunt. You walk up to the guard. He scowls at you.

"What do you want?" he says as though you are the most disgusting person alive.

"I . . . I want to report some spies," you say.

"Get out of here!" He yells. "You're a day late." He turns his back, refusing even to look at you again.

"But I have new information," you say.

The man ignores you. He walks away. You try another guard. He pushes you away. You fall backward onto the ground. The soldiers all laugh. No one will listen to your information. You give up and go home.

When you get home, you find Aunt Rahab talking with your mother. After Aunt Rahab leaves, you tell the whole family what you saw. You tell them not to believe anything Aunt Rahab says, because she is a traitor.

From then on, you and your brother Talmai practice every day with swords. You pretend you are fighting Israel. Of course, in your games Jericho always wins.

Finally, the attack comes. The wall of Jericho has fallen, and Talmai and you stand side-by-side to meet the enemy. Two Israelites are coming toward you. Your sword meets one man's with a clank. His strength surprises you. With all your might, you try to hold him off. Suddenly, Talmai falls against your leg.

"No!" you scream. You feel steel plunging into your own stomach. You both die fighting.

THE END

You decide that you can't stand feeling trapped. Your mother will eventually make up with her sister. Meanwhile, you can find out what is going on and report to everyone.

You visit Aunt Rahab every day and spend most of your time staring out the window on the city wall. You rest your elbow on the windowsill and feel something uncomfortable under it. A red cord is hanging from the window.

"What's this doing here?" you ask, starting to remove it.

Aunt Rahab panics. "No! Don't touch that! That red cord is the only way the Israelites will know where to find us." You are beginning to understand how deeply Aunt Rahab believes that she will be saved.

Soon the Israelites come into view, but not to attack. They seem to be using Jericho only for marching and music practice. You think it is funny. Lots of people in Jericho are watching from windows in the wall. After six days of this, you tell your family that Aunt Rahab's window has the best view of the parade.

"I miss my sister," your mother says. "So I'll go with you tomorrow."

Your father nods. "I've heard so much about these parades but haven't seen one yet. You say Aunt Rahab has a good view from her window?"

"The best," you say.

"Then I'll go too," your father says. "We're not doing much business at the inn now anyway. Talmai and Onan can also go."

The next day, you are all watching from Aunt Rahab's window.

"It's an odd march," your father says. "The trumpets sound, but the people are silent. They don't even sound a war cry."

"Except for those horns," your mother says. She covers her ears. Other relatives are with you. Most of them are nervous because they believe Israel is about to attack. Aunt Rahab tries to calm them with dates and fresh bread. Your fingers grow sticky.

Suddenly, the Israelites stop and look up. One is looking straight at you. They shout and the trumpets blare. A chill runs through you. Everything turns to chaos—grating noises, shaking walls, screaming villagers. You fall to the floor.

When it is over, you look out the window again. All around Aunt Rahab's house, the wall has fallen. You check to make sure the red cord is still attached. After you are rescued and taken to the Israelite camp, all of your family wants to know about Israel's God.

THE END

You and your relatives are certain that the attack will be today . . . at any moment. You are afraid that your family will not get to Aunt Rahab's in time. You ask your aunt to watch Onan, and you rush out the door.

You bump into people as you race through the streets, but you keep running.

"Are they marching again?" a voice asks.

"Of course they are," says another. "Every day it's the same silly religious parade." No one laughs. You can tell that Israel's marching is wearing on their nerves.

When you reach home, no one is there. Maybe they went to Aunt Rahab's, and you missed them on the way. You have a nagging feeling that you are wrong. Is there time to go to the inn? You must take that chance.

Your lungs feel as though they are going to burst as you fly through the inn's door. Your parents and Talmai are inside.

"Please come now!" you shout between breaths. "I've been watching the Israelites. The attack is coming, and there will be no escape! Only Aunt Rahab's house is safe!"

Your parents believe you, but your brother hesitates. You grab your brother's arm and try to drag him with you.

He pulls away. "Why shouldn't we stand and fight for our city?" he asks.

You have only one answer, and you know it is the right one, thanks to Aunt Rahab. "Because their God is the true God."

Talmai's eyes change from stubbornness to wonder, and then

instantly to fear. He grabs your hand, and you all run for Aunt Rahab's house. Just as you turn the corner onto her street, the ground begins to shake. The wall of the city is crumbling before your eyes. The door is almost within reach. You trip. Talmai picks you up, and you make it through the door just in time.

THE END

"I can't believe that you lied to the king's men," you tell Aunt Rahab. "Those spies are still here, aren't they?" You lower your voice. "Did they threaten you? I can run after the soldiers and bring them back."

"No, we don't need the soldiers. I know what I'm doing. Israel's God is powerful—not like Jericho's gods," she says. "He has helped Israel defeat mighty enemies."

You cannot believe what you are hearing. Is Aunt Rahab actually on Israel's side? You grab a grape from her table. Eating always helps you think. It is sour, though, so you grab some plumper, sweeter ones to cover the taste.

"Jericho is strong," you say. "The Israelites can't possibly get through our wall." You kick your foot against the wooden chair.

"I believe their God can help them do anything," Aunt Rahab says. "If they attack our city, they will win."

You want to think more about this, but your stomach is calling for food. "I have to go home for supper." You promise not to say anything to anyone.

During supper you are quiet. You look at each of your family members—strong Talmai, sweet Onan, your beautiful mother, and your caring father—and wonder what will happen to them if Israel attacks. After supper you rush back to Aunt Rahab's.

"Are the spies still here?" you whisper when she answers the door.

"No," Aunt Rahab says.

You breathe easier. "Tell me more about this God of Israel."

"Walls, seas, and powerful armies are no match for this God," she says. "Jericho will fall, but don't worry. Anyone who is in my house when the attack comes will be safe."

Your head is spinning. Finally you come to a decision. "I don't know why," you say, "but I believe that what you say is true." You help Aunt Rahab tie a red cord in her window.

"This cord is a sign for Israel's army," she says. "It is a secret signal to let them know where I live. When the attack comes, they will see this cord and come to rescue me and any of my father's house who are here."

"So the cord is there to help protect you?" you ask.

"Yes," Aunt Rahab says. "It will protect my house from destruction."

"Then we have to make sure that the cord doesn't come loose," you say.

"That can be your job. Will you keep checking it for me?"

You agree to go to Aunt Rahab's house every day to check the cord. When the attack comes, you are safe.

THE END

On the fifth day, you go to the inn with your father. "If you choose to die, then I'll die with you," you say. You hope he will go to Aunt Rahab's for your sake if not for his. You cook, clean, and serve meals with him.

"I saw the parade yesterday," says a customer. Others laugh as he continues, "Even my three-legged dog could beat that sorry excuse for an army."

Another customer adds, "Those cowards just walk around their enemies. Someone should tell them that it's the fighting and not the walking that wins wars." More laughter.

The first man says, "*Cowards* is the right name for them." His companions laugh, but they keep looking out the windows as if they are expecting to see Israel in their streets at any time. You sweep the floor at the end of the day and hope that your father will go to Aunt Rahab's with you the next morning.

Your father is determined to stay open for business but makes you go to Aunt Rahab's the next day with the family. You leave for Aunt Rahab's with the others. Once there, you begin to grow bored. You wonder if the Israelites really plan to attack at all. On the seventh day, you return to the inn to help your father. Business is really slow.

You are stirring food over the fire when a friend hurries in and says, "The Israelites are doing something different today. Their parade isn't just going around once. They're already on their fifth rotation." The change in the marching pattern frightens you.

"Come with me to Aunt Rahab's," you beg your father.

"We might as well," he says. Just then a customer comes into the inn and orders a leg of lamb. Your father smiles. He tells you, "Let me fill this order, and then we'll go."

"Hurry! Please hurry," you say. You go to the window and look out to the street. "Can we go now? Are you almost done?"

"A few more minutes," your father says.

The man is a slow eater. As your father sets a bowl of water on the table for the man to clean his hands, you hear people yelling outside. Then the floor begins to jiggle. Soon the earth is shaking. A deafening roar follows. You run to your father and grab his arm. The roof of the inn collapses over your heads and kills your father, his customer, and you.

THE END

◆ ◆ ◆

You do not believe the rumors. All Israel has done for the past six days is march around and blow horns. They are just noisemakers. You are laughing about it when you hear frantic knocking at the door. It is your cousins.

They pull on your arm. "Come with us to Aunt Rahab's house now. Otherwise, you will die." Onan is playing on the floor nearby. On impulse, you grab him and run to the door. You call to the rest of your family, but no one else follows. You just make it into Aunt Rahab's house when the wall of the city comes crashing down.

"How did they destroy Jericho's wall?" you ask no one in particular.

Standing at the window, your Uncle Ui says, "I don't know. I saw the whole thing, but Israel never even touched the wall. It had to be their God who destroyed it."

Maybe Israel's God is as great as people were saying! Soon Israelite soldiers come through the door and lead you to safety. You never see the rest of your family again, but you and Onan live with Aunt Rahab, and you follow the God of Israel for the rest of your lives.

THE END

After your parents leave the table, you tell Talmai, "I'll tell you everything, but first I have to fix my sandal while the light is good." Talmai helps you get the tools you need. You sit together outside the house as you work.

"You should have seen the spies today," you begin. His face brightens. You continue, "They were dressed in tan tunics with brown cloaks. I thought it was far too warm for the cloaks. That's what made me suspect them at once. They had their heads covered, but I could see that one of them had curly hair."

"How did you know they were Israelites?"

"I heard two men in Jericho talking about them. They said something about the Israelites' powerful God drowning the whole Egyptian army."

You place a leather strap in your mouth to stretch it. When the strap looks right, you spit it out and get a drink of water to rinse out the leather taste. You say, "I think they were exaggerating, don't you?"

He nods. "But what about Aunt Rahab? Is she really in danger?"

"She might be." You look up to make sure your parents are not around and lower your voice. "The spies went into her house."

Just then your father walks up the street toward you. "What are you two troublemakers doing?"

Instead of answering, you say, "I already fed the livestock." He nods. You both follow him inside your house. The lamb from earlier has been cut up and is cooking over the fire into some type of soup for tomorrow. You like it when the house smells like this.

"Israelite spies were seen in the city today," your father says to no one in particular, "but they've gone. The king's men are giving chase."

"I wish I could have gone with the king's men," Talmai says.

"I would have liked to watch the chase from the top of the wall," you add.

"You have enough to do helping out around here," says your father. "Which reminds me. I need both of you to work at the inn tomorrow before we open for business." You groan.

The next morning, you have just returned from the inn when Aunt Rahab comes to visit.

Before she can tell you hello, Talmai asks in a loud voice, "What was it like to have spies in your house?" She seems surprised that you know about her visitors.

"Is it true that their God opened the sea for them to walk through and then drowned the whole Egyptian army?" you ask. "Our gods have never done anything like that."

"That's because our gods are made by people," Aunt Rahab says. "They're just metal, wood, or rocks—like the ones that you kick around. They have no power. But Israel's God is alive! I believe He is the only true God."

Your mother drops the bowl of beans she is preparing. The bowl does not crack, but beans are everywhere. You are glad your father is at the inn. He would not like this kind of talk. You all help your mother gather the spilled beans.

Onan grabs a handful and toddles away with them, giggling. You chase him and take the beans from his hands. You give him two rocks to play with and set him on your lap. You stick a bean in your mouth and enjoy its fresh, crunchy flavor.

Aunt Rahab now directs her words to your mother. "Shebna, you have to believe me. Israel's God is going to destroy Jericho. Everyone who is not inside my house during the battle will be killed. Promise that you will come to my house."

Your mother's eyebrows draw together. "I'll think about it, Rahab, but I won't promise. I must talk this over with my husband." Aunt Rahab smiles and leaves.

CHOICE ONE: If you do not believe what Aunt Rahab says, go to page 116.

CHOICE TWO: If you believe what Aunt Rahab says, go to page 93.

Attack!

A warm breeze makes your tunic flutter as you stand on a grassy hillside near Judah's border. When the enemy comes, you will be ready. You swallow the last chunk of bread from the leather pouch at your side. The peaceful bleating of your family's sheep makes it hard to believe that war could break out soon. Three armies, including the neighboring Edomites, plan to attack—at least that's what you've heard.

You choose several smooth stones for your sling. With God's help, you're sure to beat the enemy, just as King David did almost one hundred years ago when he killed Goliath.

Was that a noise? It sounded like someone stepping on loose stones. You study the rocks and plants on the hillside across from you. Was that movement in the distance?

Your heart races and your throat tightens. You don't know if you're ready to fight the enemy all by yourself. Everything is silent. You are afraid even to breathe. Suddenly, something leaps from behind a boulder. Whew! It was only a rabbit.

You fill your scrip—the leather pouch that held your lunch—with rocks. Then you sit down. Maybe it is silly to worry about the enemy. You live in such a little town; they probably won't even bother to attack here. You pick up your kinnor and gently strum it. Your great-grandfather played this U-shaped harp in the Temple at Jerusalem when Solomon was king. You have just begun to sing one of David's psalms when suddenly two strong arms pull you backward. Other arms tear your instrument from you.

You cringe, waiting to die, until you see the faces of Joash and his friends. You try to pull away from them, but their arms hold you tightly.

"Stop it!" you yell. One of the boys has your kinnor. "Give it back!"

Joash jumps on top of you and sits on your stomach. He is bigger and stronger. Your back is pressed against sharp rocks, and your eyes look up into a blue-gray sky.

"Some watcher you are," Joash says. "You didn't even hear us coming." One of Joash's friends sneers, "And you were scared of a tiny rabbit."

"I was not," you say. "I was just—"

Joash covers your mouth with his hands. "We saw you jump. You're too much of a baby to protect sheep. Your father just sends you out here so no one will have to listen to your squeaky voice or the awful music you make." Joash smells worse than the dirt-caked wool on your sheep.

His friends toss your kinnor back and forth between them. You don't want them to break it, but you can't say anything with Joash's stinky hand in your face.

"You're not even worth fighting." Joash pushes his weight down on you as he stands up.

"Just wait until the attack comes," you say, sitting up. "I'll fight for Judah as hard as the bravest soldier."

"You? You're too scrawny to hold a real weapon."

You roll to the side and grab your rod to hit Joash, but as soon as it is in your hand, one of his friends kicks it to the ground. You hate how helpless they make you feel.

"You can't even handle a rod," Joash taunts. "All you're good for is watching tame sheep." He laughs. "What an ugly instrument." He takes your kinnor from the others and tosses it high into the air.

"Don't! That belongs to my family," you yell. "Give it back now or I'll tell my father."

Joash smiles. "If you want your old harp, come and get it." He and his friends run down the other side of the hill, throwing it wildly between them. You feel the blood rising in your face and breathe deeply to keep from yelling the wrong words after them.

You want your kinnor back, but you are supposed to be watching the sheep. Your brother is going to relieve you soon. A figure in the distance looks like it could be Reuben, but you can't be certain.

CHOICE ONE: If you wave to the person in the distance and then chase after Joash, go to page 172.

CHOICE TWO: If you stay with the sheep and then later tell your parents what happened, go to page 173.

CHOICE THREE: If you follow the bullies while trying to keep an eye on your sheep, go to page 175.

◆ ◆ ◆

You stare into the distance. The person is wearing a light-colored robe like your brother's, and his hair is dark. *It has to be Reuben,* you think. You wave your hands in the air in a large circle. When you feel certain that Reuben sees you, you tie up your robe and run after Joash and his friends.

They head over the ridge. Instead of running directly after them, you take a shortcut and skirt the hills to cut them off. A pebble slides into your sandal, but you can't stop to remove it. Timing is everything. You would rather ignore the sharp lump under your arch if it means you will get your kinnor back.

The sound of laughter and scuffling feet to your left tell you that you were correct. They are heading toward the caves. From a cleft in the rock, you jump out. Joash looks startled. "Where did you come from?" Without a word, you lunge at the kinnor. Thinking quickly, Joash steps to the side. Your fingers grab empty air. Off balance, you fall to the hard ground. As your head hits the dirt, the jolt makes you bite your lip.

Ignoring the taste of blood, you say, "Give it back!"

"Come and get it!" Joash yells, tossing it to a friend.

One of them says, "This way!" You stand up as they slide down the hill to a cave. Their laughter echoes as they go inside. You hurry to the cave entrance, where the air smells stale and feels stagnant.

CHOICE ONE: If you follow them into the cave,
go to page 176.

CHOICE TWO: If you mark the cave to find it later and
then hurry back to the sheep, go to page 179.

◆ ◆ ◆

Although you are afraid that you will never see your kinnor again, you do not run after Joash. You must stay with the sheep. Your family is depending on you to keep them safe. When the person in the distance disappears in another direction, you are glad you did not mistake the traveler for Reuben. By the time Reuben gets to you, Joash is long gone.

That night over a meal of vegetables and barley bread, you tell your parents what happened. When you are finished eating, they take you to Joash's house. You knock on the wooden door. Joash's father fills the doorway.

Your father says, "Pardon the intrusion, but our child accuses your son of stealing our family's kinnor."

You can't wait for Joash to get what he deserves. You can smell lentil stew in the air as you are invited inside. They probably just finished cleaning up after their evening meal.

"Joash, come here," his father says. "Did you take this family's kinnor?" Joash shakes his head no. He puts on a humble expression. You feel like hitting him.

"No, Father," he says. "I was with the rabbi all day. My friends were with me. They will tell you."

Your father smiles apologetically. "We're sorry to have disturbed you." You can't believe that your father would give up so easily.

Your father's smile tightens, and you know you should not speak. But when you are away from Joash's house, you say, "He *did* take my kinnor." Your father remains silent. It is a quiet walk back to your house.

Once inside, your father says, "You lost it, didn't you? We told you over and over to be careful with that kinnor. I should have waited to give it to you until you were older and more responsible."

"Is it possible that you broke the kinnor and are afraid to tell us?" your mother asks. "Don't be afraid to tell the truth. Lying is much worse than a broken kinnor. Once when I was a girl, I broke my mother's favorite bowl and then made up a tale about how it was stolen. The lies kept growing until I was eventually found out."

"I didn't lose or break it," you say. "Joash stole it."

"I want the truth from you," your father says.

"I *am* telling the truth."

Your mother looks at you sadly and sighs. "We're glad that you stayed with the sheep."

Your parents stop talking about the kinnor, but you can tell that they think you lied to them. You are so angry that they are taking Joash's word over yours that you decide to run away.

CHOICE ONE: If you run as fast and as far away as you can go, turn to page 180.

CHOICE TWO: If you hide in the caves for a few days to give your parents a chance to change their minds, go to page 182.

Even as you start to run after Joash, you wonder whether you should be chasing him or watching your sheep. You are torn. You hope you can do both.

"Joash, I'll tell your father if you don't give it back right now!" you yell.

"Tattletale!" he calls back. You stub your sandal on the uneven ground.

"If you give it back to me right now," you yell, "I'll take your turn watching your family's sheep." You look back at your sheep to make sure they are okay. Then you continue the chase.

"You'd only get me into trouble," he yells. He tosses your kinnor to one of his friends. The instrument gives a soft whirring sound while flying through the air. His friend catches it and then tosses the kinnor back. The instrument makes an abrupt twang when Joash grabs it. To you, it sounds like a cry for help.

"You are going to be in big trouble if you don't give it to me right now," you yell. You look back at your sheep. They seem okay, but when you can't smell their scent on the breeze, you know you are too far away.

You turn your attention to the boys in time to see Joash throw your kinnor high into the air.

CHOICE ONE: If you sprint and try to catch it,
go to page 183.

CHOICE TWO: If you yell at him, go to page 185.

◆ ◆ ◆

You hurry into the cave so that you won't lose them. The darkness blinds you, and you have to stop to let your eyes adjust to your surroundings. As you wait, you listen. You hear dripping water and faint squeaking sounds. You duck out of the way of a sudden fluttering of wings. A cold shiver runs down your spine. You wish you had your cloak.

In the distance, you hear muffled panting and laughter. It seems to be coming from your right. You move farther into the cave, letting your hand trail along the stone edges. The walls feel cool. In some spots, they are damp and almost slimy. You let go of the walls and pull your arms closer to your body.

Something is crawling up your arm. You stifle a scream and brush off the creature. You do not want Joash to know you are following him or that you are scared. Unable to handle the bugs, you spin around to leave, but the thought of a broken kinnor makes you change your mind. With a sigh, you move once again in the direction of the laughter.

Everything is silent now. Just then, something drops on your head. You close your eyes and clench your fists until you feel wetness dripping down your scalp. It is only water. You take a deep breath and proceed, trying not to think about the spiders and other creatures above and all around you.

You turn a sharp corner. A dim shaft of light from above shines directly on an enormous spider in front of you. Your scream echoes through the cave as you duck to get away from it. In your haste, you slip on loose rocks and lose your balance. Your left foot gets wedged between the stones. Other rocks slip around your ankle.

A sharp pain runs up your leg as you try to pull out your foot. It will not budge. The spider hovers above you in the cave's only sliver of dim light. Your skin feels as though it is crawling with bugs. Are they real, or are you imagining them? Either way, you have to get out of there fast! You pull harder to free your foot, biting your tunic to keep from yelling in pain. The wool gags you. Your ankle is at a dangerous angle, and you are afraid you will break it if you are not careful.

CHOICE ONE: If you pray and ask God for help,
go to page 203.

CHOICE TWO: If you begin yelling for help,
go to page 205.

◆ ◆ ◆

You have to get back to the sheep, so you take a soft stone and mark the cave opening. That way you will be able to find the entrance again and search for your kinnor later tonight.

You hurry back to the field where the sheep are still grazing. They look so peaceful. Reuben has not yet arrived. The person you saw in the distance must have been a traveler, not your brother. You circle the sheep to warn predators that the flock is under your protection.

When your brother finally comes to relieve you, you hurry home as fast as you can and tell your parents what happened.

Your father says, "We gave you that kinnor because we thought you were old enough to take care of it."

You try to explain. "But Joash and his friends—"

"I am very disappointed in you," your father says. You realize that your father thinks the kinnor is lost forever.

That night, you wait for everyone to fall asleep before you sneak out with a small clay lamp. You are going to find your kinnor! You go to the spot where you think you saw Joash enter the caves, but you can't find your mark. Joash could have entered either of the two caves in front of you.

CHOICE ONE: If you enter the cave entrance on the left, go to page 217.

CHOICE TWO: If you enter the cave entrance on the right, go to page 219.

When your mother is in the house and your father has turned his attention to other things, you casually move toward the road and then boldly walk away from your village. You do not look back. When you have walked for a while, you throw back your head and begin to run. If your family will not believe the truth, maybe strangers will.

You want to get as far away as you can. You run and run as the sky darkens. Although you were tired earlier, you seem to have new strength now. You run for a long time. Tears blind your eyes. You taste their salt streaming into your mouth. You can't see clearly in front of you. Your side aches, but you keep running until you are too exhausted to think. Hours pass in a darkness where only the sound of your breathing reaches your ears.

The air no longer smells familiar, but you do not stop. You keep running. Your emotions carry you forward. The scent in the air grows stronger. You follow it until you see campfires in the distance. You head toward them, hoping to find bread, water, and a warm place to rest. Just in time, you real2ize that you have happened upon the camp of the Ammonite, Edomite, and Moabite armies. These are the ones getting ready to attack Judah! One of the sentries looks in your direction. You drop to the ground, hoping he didn't see you in the darkness.

He moves toward you with his weapon raised. You slide on your stomach over pebbles and prickly plants to get away from the place where he might have seen you. Each time he stops moving to listen, you lie completely still so he doesn't hear you move. Prickles are digging into your stomach.

"Stand up, you coward, and come here, or I'll kill you where you lie!" He is looking directly at you.

CHOICE ONE: If you stand up and ask for mercy,
go to page 190.

CHOICE TWO: If you stay where you are and do not
move, go to page 192.

In the night, you take some of your family's food and your cloak. You go to the caves not far from your village and hide.

I'll stay away long enough to make them feel sorry for not believing me, you tell yourself. You live in a cave for three days. Finally, you grow tired of being alone. You have eaten all your food. You decide to go home.

When you get back, your village is empty. Everyone is gone. You go from house to house, wondering what has happened. From a neighbor's window, you see foreign soldiers searching other homes. You realize that the rumors of war are true.

You hurry out of the house without stopping to take any food. You ignore your growling stomach, craving only the safety of the caves.

In your haste to get back to the cave, you fall and cut your leg. You stifle your cries of pain to keep the foreigners from discovering you. Fortunately, you are able to make it back to your hiding place without being seen.

Your cut keeps bleeding. You put pressure on it, but it won't stop. You suddenly feel weak from the loss of blood and lack of food. You lie down on your cloak to rest. You fall asleep. When you wake up, a crust of dried blood has formed over your wound, but it throbs and feels hot to the touch.

In the middle of the night, you can't move your leg without it hurting. By morning, you are delirious with fever and can't move to get food or water. The infection in your leg eventually spreads into your blood. One night you fall asleep and never wake up.

THE END

◆ ◆ ◆

You sprint toward the airborne kinnor. Every muscle in your body is tensed in your effort to reach it before it falls to the ground. You don't know if you can catch it, but you have to try. Your hand stretches up into the air. It's as if the world is moving in slow motion for you. Suddenly, the kinnor stops moving upward and begins falling. You aren't close enough! You are afraid you won't get there in time. Joash's laughter sounds far off and distorted.

You feel yourself leave the ground and fly in the direction of your instrument. And then it happens! The kinnor touches the edge of your hand. You have just enough strength to grab it and pull it close to you before you tumble to the ground. It's safe! You are a little scraped up, but relieved. Your heart pumps fast, and you stay where you are to catch your breath. You look up. Joash is there. For a second he looks relieved, then his usual taunting returns.

"You're so lame." He spins around and takes off, catching up with his friends.

Just then, you remember the sheep. You can't see them from where you are. You stand and race up the hill. You breathe a quick "Thank you, God" when you see them grazing peacefully.

As you sit and watch the sheep, you jump at every sound. You are afraid that Joash and his followers will come back. You hold your kinnor tightly to your chest. You didn't realize how important it was to you until you almost lost it. It is a precious part of your family's history.

After a while, you see Joash and his friends coming back.

"What do you want?" you ask, moving away from them.

"We don't want you to play your kinnor or sing out here anymore," Joash says.

His friend adds, "We don't like your squeaky voice."

"And what if I sing anyway?"

Joash's face turns threatening. "Next time, you won't get your kinnor back." He turns to his friends. "We've wasted enough time here. Let's go."

As they run off, you sigh.

CHOICE ONE: If you decide never to sing or play your kinnor in front of Joash again, go to page 235.

CHOICE TWO: If you get back at Joash for bullying you, go to page 236.

The kinnor lands and breaks. Rage fills you, and you completely forget about your sheep. You jump up and run after Joash with your fists raised. He starts running. You chase him for miles without thinking about how tired you are.

Joash stops without warning, and you run into him. You back up to catch your breath and prepare for his assault.

He says, "We're in trouble." He points. You look in the direction where he is pointing and see thousands of foreign-looking tents. They go on for as far as you can see.

Your anger vanishes. "Who are they?" You move closer to Joash.

He shakes his head. "The rumors must be true. How can Judah ever win against an army as big as that?"

"What should we do?" you ask.

"I don't know," Joash says. "You're the smart one. What do you think we should do?"

You try not to look startled at the compliment. "Maybe we can find out their plans and warn Judah."

He nods. "Let's sneak along the ridge that overlooks those tents. They're bigger than the others and probably belong to the leaders."

"Okay." Quietly you begin moving toward the ridge. You mimic Joash's movements, and now you understand why you never heard him coming. Joash is good at staying hidden, and he's as silent as a fox.

When you get to the edge of the ridge, you point to the steep side to show Joash where to go. He nods. You both work your way down, helping each other. A few times, dirt and stones slide down ahead of you. You try to move more carefully.

When you reach the base of the ridge, you hear sentries talking on the other side of a large rock, but you can't quite make out what they are saying. Joash puts his hand up to let you know he's listening. When he gives you the signal, you move to a place where you can whisper together.

Joash says, "The first man wanted to know when they will attack us. He thinks they have plenty of soldiers already. The other one says that they are waiting for another army to join them. What should we do now?"

CHOICE ONE: If you leave to warn your village, go to page 193.

CHOICE TWO: If you stay to find out more about the enemy's plans, go to page 195.

You try to cooperate with the soldier, but his flashing eyes scare you. As his questions become more intense, he puts his face right in front of yours. His breath smells like old garlic and rotten teeth. You remind yourself that he is trying to help you. You just want to go home.

"I don't know anything else," you say. "I've told you everything I know. I'd tell you more if I knew more."

The soldier sits and gazes out into the distance. You wonder what he is thinking. Perhaps it is about his son.

"You have betrayed your country," he says simply. "Traitors don't deserve to live." His words surprise you.

He stands up and draws his sword from its sheath. It gleams in the sunlight.

"Oh no!" you say. "But your son is my age. You said that—"

"I'm a soldier," he says. "I don't have any children. You've betrayed the people you love, so you will betray your enemies."

You whisper, "God, please forgive me," just before the soldier kills you.

THE END

You say, "I won't tell you a thing. The God of Judah is stronger than you and your army, and you will regret the day that you chose to mess with God's people."

"You insignificant brat," the soldier says. He returns his sword to its sheath. "You don't understand the power we have. Just look out there at the many armies."

"And you don't know the power of my God," you say. You close your eyes, expecting to feel his sword strike you.

"Killing you would be too easy," says the soldier. "I'm going to keep you alive as my slave. When you have seen your people destroyed and your God shamed, then I will kill you."

You shrug. You don't want him to know how scared you are. From that time on, you have to fetch and clean and carry things for this soldier. He eats chunks of meat and fresh bread that make your mouth water. You are only allowed to eat whatever scraps he leaves behind. He beats you every day.

When the army changes its position, your life is especially hard. You have to carry more than your own weight. Although the man is cruel, you try to honor God by the way you behave toward him.

At night, you remember your family, and you miss them. You are sorry for running away. You dream of home and pray that God will help you return someday.

One morning you wake up to the sound of shouting, scuffling, and screaming. You wonder what the commotion is. You stay in your tent. The battle must have begun. The clank of metal grates on your nerves. You hear a moan just outside the tent, and someone falls against it. You crawl into the middle of the tent, trying to hold your trembling body still with your arms. You wonder why you ever wanted to fight for Judah. This is not the romantic idea you had about the life of a soldier. There are too many sounds of metal scraping metal and groans of pain. It might be your imagination, but the smell of sweat mixed with blood reaches your nostrils.

Finally, you must know what is happening. You pull back the tent flap and hold it in a clenched fist. Fighting soldiers and dead bodies are everywhere. The sun is still low in the morning sky. This could be your chance to escape, but you aren't sure if you have the courage to try it.

CHOICE ONE: If you stay in the tent, go to page 238.

CHOICE TWO: If you try to escape, go to page 239.

◆ ◆ ◆

"I give up!" you yell as you slowly stand up.

"Get over here," the soldier demands roughly.

"I don't have a weapon." You walk slowly toward the man. He is even bigger than you imagined. When you reach him, he pushes you toward the camp.

"Where are you taking me?" you ask.

"Be quiet!" he demands. He forces you toward one of the tents and then tosses you inside. It is empty. You hear voices outside, but they are talking so low that you can't understand what they are saying. You hurry to the back of the goat-hair tent and grope at the edges next to the ground. You hope to find a loose area so you can escape, but the entire tent is pegged firmly with tent nails.

When the voices quiet, you dive back to the center of the tent. The soldier ducks to enter, and you see faint rays of the rising sun behind him.

"You are an enemy spy. You must die." His sword scrapes against its sheath as he draws it out.

"Mercy, please!" you cry as you kneel before him. "I don't know anything about spying."

The soldier pauses and gives you a long look. "You are about the age of my son." With a sigh, he slides his sword back into its sheath.

As if disgusted with himself, he grabs the back of your clothes and drags you. You keep trying to scramble to your feet. You taste the wool of your tunic in your mouth and remember how lovingly your mother wove it. You grow angry at the man for handling it so roughly. His sword clanks as he walks. When you reach a rise above the camp, he stops and drops you to the ground.

You raise your head and stare at the enemy tents before you. They stretch as far as you can see. Judah can never defeat this vast army.

"I must kill you," the soldier says, "unless we can find some way that you can be useful to us. Can you cook for a thousand men?"

"Uh. No."

"You're too scrawny to carry equipment. There is nothing you can do. I'll have to kill you," he says. "I'm sorry."

"Wait!" you exclaim. "There has to be something I can do."

"Are you willing to give us information about your country and its army?"

You hesitate, thinking about all the people back in your town. But how can little Judah win against such a multitude?

The man continues. "Look around you. Whether you tell us anything or not, we will take over your country. But if you help us, I might be able to save your family."

"Like Israel did for Rahab when Jericho fell?" you ask. Then you remember that God was on Israel's side when Jericho fell.

The soldier shrugs. "I don't know anything about that. If you join us, you'll save yourself, your family, and maybe your whole village."

CHOICE ONE: If you tell the soldier what he wants to know, go to page 187.

CHOICE TWO: If you refuse to tell the soldier anything, go to page 188.

◆ ◆ ◆

Y ou do not move. You barely breathe. You hear footsteps.
"Who are you yelling at?" asks a rough voice.

"I thought I saw something," the soldier says. "It must have been a small animal, or else my mind is playing tricks on me."

"Your shift is over," says the first voice. "I'll take your place."

You hear footsteps walking away.

You continue moving forward, pushing with your toes. Inch by inch, you crawl to rocks that overlook the camp. There is a tent directly below you and a crevice where you can hide under the shelter of a rock. A trickle of a stream flows through the crevice, and a tiny pool has gathered on a small ledge. The moon shimmers on the water. You drink from the pool and then fall asleep.

You awake when you hear voices. "In two days, we should attack Judah!"

"No!" says another angry voice. "We must wait for the rest of the Moabites to join us. They will be here soon."

"You've been saying that for days!"

Someone taps you on the shoulder. You look up, alarmed. A child is looking down at you. He puts his index finger to his mouth for you to be quiet.

He whispers, "I am a slave at this camp. Come with me. If you stay here, they will find you."

CHOICE ONE: If you go with the slave, go to page 227.

CHOICE TWO: If you run away from the slave,
go to page 230.

You motion toward the ridge, and Joash nods his understanding. It takes a long time, but you help each other up the cleft in the ridge. Suddenly, your foot catches a loose stone that tumbles off the ledge. Thinking quickly, Joash catches it before it falls to the ground.

You mouth, "Thanks," to him. He gives you a quick smile.

Just then two sentries come into view below you. Before they look up, you both give one last push to make it over the rim undetected. You lie on top of it, and feel yourself shaking. That was too close.

After you have had a moment to rest, you slowly pick your way through the underbrush, away from the camp. You are surprised at how well you both work together.

Once you are far enough away not to be seen or heard, you say, "We have to warn our village."

"And Jerusalem," Joash adds.

"I'll warn the village," you say.

"And I'll take Jerusalem," Joash says. "May God be with you."

"And with you," you say. You know that Joash has a lot farther to run than you do. Without another word, you give each other a hug. You are in this together.

You run in different directions. Licking the dirt from your lips, you race for home. By the time you return to your village, everyone is packing to go to Jerusalem. While you were gone, a messenger from King Jehoshaphat commanded all of Judah to come to Jerusalem to fast and pray for victory over the enemy.

"I've seen the army, and Joash is on his way to Jerusalem," you tell your parents, the elders, and Joash's parents. You answer questions about what you and Joash saw. Your news only makes the villagers move more swiftly. You leave as a group for the city.

For such a large group, you are surprised at how quiet everyone is. Not even the children are talking much. Only the sounds of sheep and goats bleating, with an occasional barking dog, fill the air.

When you get to Jerusalem days later, you see Joash in the distance. You are about to wave to him when you notice that he is wearing a soldier's uniform. You are jealous. You are the one who wanted to fight for Judah.

CHOICE ONE: If you avoid Joash, go to page 198.

CHOICE TWO: If you talk to Joash, go to page 199.

You decide to find out more about the enemy's plans so that you can report them to the king in Jerusalem. As you move closer, you step on a rock and slip. The sound draws the sentries to you.

Joash jumps between you and the sentries.

"Run!" he yells to you. "Run!" He flings himself in their way. You take off before other soldiers arrive. You may be small, but you're quick. After all, you kept up with Joash on the way to this camp. You keep telling yourself that to keep up your courage.

Only once do you glance behind you. Joash's limp body is lying on the ground, and soldiers are chasing you. You can't let him die for nothing. He gave his life to help you get away. You run harder than you have ever run. You do not look back. You breathe deeply from the fresh air around you.

You do not want the enemy to follow you to your village, so you head straight for Jerusalem. Although the enemy stops chasing you once you get deep into Judah's territory, you keep running as if Joash were after you. From all his years of bullying you, he has trained you for this important run. You do not stop until you reach Jerusalem.

"I've just come from the enemy camp," you gasp. "Take me to the king." Someone gives you water, and you relish its coolness in your mouth and throat. Once you tell King Jehoshaphat about everything you have seen and about what happened to Joash, you pass out from exhaustion.

When you wake up, many days have passed. Your parents are with you, and Judah's battle is over. The enemy is no more! Although you

are content to be with your family, you will never forget what Joash did for you. You just wish you could have saved his life. You might have become good friends.

THE END

◆ ◆ ◆

You feel as if you've eaten bitter herbs. You quickly duck behind your parents and smell the dust in your mother's traveling robe. Joash is not your friend. He never was. It was your dream to march beside the army, not his.

If you had chosen to warn Jerusalem instead of the village, you would be with the soldiers now instead of Joash. Whenever you see him in the distance, you turn down a different street. For two days, Joash tries to find you.

Your mother says, "Joash came by again."

Your father says, "Go see Joash. I keep running into him, and he asks about you. We were praying together today. Where were you?"

"I was around," you say with a shrug, but you are determined not to meet with Joash. You duck behind people and hide in stinky animal carts to get away from him.

Before long, you watch as Joash marches into battle with the army. Joash has stolen more than just your kinnor. He has stolen all your dreams. Life is unfair.

You despise Joash. With every year that goes by, you become more and more bitter. You grow up mean and grumpy.

THE END

◆ ◆ ◆

Y ou are so jealous that you can hardly bear to see Joash. Ignoring your jealous feelings, you take a deep breath and face him.

"My friend!" he says in greeting and gives you an enormous hug. He pulls you along after him and introduces you to so many soldiers that you can't remember all their names.

Each person whom you are introduced to says, "Sing for us." You are surprised at their request.

"I told them what a great singer you are," Joash says sheepishly.

"I thought you hated my singing."

Joash kicks the ground. "Actually, I was jealous of it."

"You were?"

"Yeah. I can hardly carry a tune. I'd really like it if you would sing for all of us. When you sing and worship God with your voice, I like the way it makes me feel. It's almost as if God is there too."

You sing for them. They really seem to appreciate it, so you sing everything you know. They thank you when you are done. Days later when you see them marching out of the city, you are glad that you sang. You know they will need God's help.

When the army marches back into Jerusalem many days later, one of the Temple singers asks your parents if you can stay and work under him as his servant. He has heard the soldiers raving about your voice. Your parents agree. Both you and Joash remain in Jerusalem, and you become lifelong friends.

THE END

"I don't usually sing for people," you say, "but I'll try." You close your eyes and tell God, "I need Your help to do this." Out loud, you say, "You almost carried me all the way home. Singing for you is the least I can do."

Simeon's warm smile encourages you. You feel God's peace as you begin to play. You sing a psalm of praise that you learned from your father. When you finish singing, the house is quiet. You open your eyes. There are tears on your mother's cheeks. Your father's usually stern face has softened.

"Thank you," Simeon says. "That was beautiful. I feel refreshed."

You nod, a little embarrassed by his praise.

The next morning, the elders of your village gather to hear the king's message. Your father is in his best robes, and your mother has dabbed on a small amount of nard. She smells like sweet honey.

Simeon tells the village that King Jehoshaphat has called all of Judah to come to Jerusalem to fast and pray. The rumors are true. A huge attack is coming. Judah's enemies could strike any day.

The people of the village quickly pack food, clothing, and other necessities for the journey. Some are afraid to leave their valuables behind. They take everything they can carry. As you help your family pack, you remember how you fought the wolf. Somehow you feel braver than before. You wonder if you should stay behind to guard the village. You seldom miss with your slingshot.

CHOICE ONE: If you stay and protect your village,
go to page 221.

CHOICE TWO: If you leave with your family, go to page 223.

The kinnor always brings you peace and comfort, and you want to play it. But what if your voice comes out squeaky like Joash said it does? You shake your head. "I'm sorry, but the dampness in the cave wasn't good for my voice. I think I should rest it. Perhaps another time."

Simeon smiles, "Of course."

You feel guilty about making excuses. You go for a walk, carrying your kinnor with you to a lonely spot near the edge of town. Sitting down where you do not think anyone will hear you, you begin to play and sing.

Instead of feeling peace, you feel ashamed. Just after you decide to go back and sing for Simeon, you feel Joash's arms around you again. He yanks your kinnor from your fingers. This time, you can't run after him. Your ankle hurts too much. You do not even try.

You limp home and help your parents prepare for the trip to Jerusalem. Your family leaves with a large group of others from the village.

One night on the way to Jerusalem, you go for a walk. Your ankle is feeling much better. You hear music in the distance. It sounds like some kind of harp. Quietly, you try to sneak up on whoever is playing it, not wanting to disturb the musician.

You hide behind a rock and peer around the edge of it. Joash is strumming your kinnor!

You rush out and say, "What are you doing?" Joash stands up as if to flee. When you do not move closer, he stays where he is.

"I'm playing," he says defiantly. This does not make sense, and you wonder for a minute if you are dreaming. Joash likes music?

You want to say something mean to get back at him for taking your kinnor, but you recognize the embarrassment in his eyes. Instead, you say, "Your playing sounded good, but I could teach you to play even better."

Joash looks at you uncertainly. Only the night breeze fills the silence between you until you say, "If you give me back my kinnor, we can find a place to practice every night."

"It'll be a secret, right?"

You nod. He gives you the kinnor with a sheepish smile. You hold it close to your chest.

"You're okay," he says.

"So are you," you say. "But why did you take so long to show it?"

He shrugs. You walk back to camp together.

THE END

◆ ◆ ◆

"God of my fathers," you pray. "Please help me. If I don't die from bug bites, I'll eventually die from thirst and starvation." You feel God's peace settle on you and realize that you were panicking.

"Thank you, God," you say. Carefully, you twist your body to find a position where your ankle will not hurt. As you grab at the wall, your hand slips, and a rock tumbles over a ledge. It echoes as it hits bottom far below. You shiver. In the darkness, you try to concentrate on God's power instead of hairy spiders and dangerous pits.

Suddenly, you have an idea. You untie the sandal straps from around your ankle. Once the leather is released, you are able to gently slide your foot from beneath the rocks.

"Thank you, God," you say. Your foot hurts but you know you will be okay. Slowly you work the rough leather of your sandal free and tie it back onto your foot. A fine dust makes you sneeze.

You reach for a rock ledge on the wall to pull yourself up. As your hand slides onto it, you touch the edge of your kinnor. Your fingers quickly find the strings. Their gentle sound echoes in the passage. You realize that you would never have found your kinnor if your foot had not been wedged beneath the stones.

You wrap the kinnor in one of your arms and test your weight on your injured foot. You think you can work the kinks out of it. Limping, you slowly feel your way back to the entrance.

The light outside pierces your eyes. Shielding your face, you hobble as fast as you can back to your flock. When you reach them, a wolf leaps out, growling. It blocks your way to the sheep. You do not see Reuben anywhere.

CHOICE ONE: If you don't want to fight the wolf,
go to page 209.

CHOICE TWO: If you attack the wolf, go to page 210.

◆ ◆ ◆

"Help! Help!" you yell. No one hears you. You yell for hours. Your voice grows hoarse. You can barely hear your last "Help!" before you decide to rest your voice.

You try to overcome your fear of the crawling creatures and lean against the wall. To find a more comfortable position, you pull yourself up and stretch your free leg. Your hand touches something that does not feel like a rock. It is your kinnor! You slide it off a ledge and hug it to yourself. It feels as though you have found an old friend. You hold it up and begin to strum. Perhaps the music will float down the passage and draw someone in to investigate. You play it for some time, and the music comforts you.

"Is someone in there?" calls a deep voice.

"Yes. Help, I'm stuck," you yell as well as you can. Your voice cracks, "I'm over here." You play your instrument to guide him. A face appears in the shaft of light near the spiderweb.

"I'm Simeon," he says. He uses his staff as a lever to free your foot from the rocks.

As he helps you home, you find out that this important-looking man has a message for your town from King Jehoshaphat. You sneeze. Your head feels stuffy, you have a headache, and you feel a cough coming on.

"It was damp in that cave," Simeon says. "It's not really a good place to practice, you know."

You do not explain what you were doing in the cave. When you get home, you limp to the shelf where you usually keep the kinnor and put it away. You do not want to risk having Joash steal it again.

It is too precious to you and your family. From now on, you will only make pipes out of reeds to play when you are watching the sheep. Joash has already broken two, but they are easy to make. You are a little disappointed that you will not be able to sing and play at the same time, but you will do anything you need to do to keep your family's kinnor safe.

THE END

◆ ◆ ◆

A horror of dying washes over you.

"God, is this true?" you ask. "Help me to know."

God has made you a singer, and the king has appointed you to go ahead of the army with the greatest singers in Judah. You do not want to die, but you know what you must do. Praising God is even better than defending your country. Whatever happens, you will march into battle for God and for Judah.

As you join the singers and begin the march toward the desert of Tekoa and the enemy, your heart beats faster. Simeon's master gives a signal, and you all begin singing, "Give thanks to the Lord, for his love endures forever." Like King David of old, you are both a soldier and a singer. You are surprised that your dream has come true in a way you could not have imagined.

The singing continues, louder and louder, as you approach the enemy camp. Suddenly, the singers in front of you halt. You move ahead of them to see why. As you sing, you stare down into the gorge where the enemy should be preparing to fight you. As far as you can see are enemy soldiers, thousands of them, but not one is standing. They are all dead. A loud cheer moves through the forces. You sing praises to God even louder than before.

God defeated Judah's enemies before your arrival! All that is left to do is to divide the enemy's things and take them home to your families. There is so much that it takes three days to gather it all. On the fourth day, you have a big praise party to thank God for His victory. Then you all march joyfully back to Jerusalem.

THE END

◆ ◆ ◆

If Joash is telling the truth, then you will die.

You are afraid to die. You slip away from the crowds and hide between the temporary camp and Jerusalem's wall. You lean against the hard surface, away from the squeeze of the crowd and the smell of sweaty people.

When the singers pass through the gates, the soldiers follow them. They look so majestic with all their weapons. You wish you had enough courage to take part in that assembly. If only you had not been chosen as one of Judah's sacrificial lambs!

Then you notice that Joash is an arms bearer for the soldiers. He sees you and smirks.

At that moment, you know he was lying. Jehaziel's words come back to you. God said that Judah would win the battle. How could you have forgotten that, even for a second? If you had taken your place up front with the singers, you would have seen God's victory firsthand. How could you have been such a fool? You vow never to let fear rule your life again. You walk back to where your family is staying.

Eventually, the battle is won, and the fast is over. But not even your mother's bread satisfies you. You regret your cowardly decision for the rest of your life.

THE END

The wolf slinks toward the flock. Your rod, sling, and scrip full of stones lie nearby. You can't let the wolf kill one of your sheep. You put down the kinnor and grab your rod. Ignoring the throbbing in your injured foot, you chase after the wolf. Suddenly, you slip and twist your ankle again. The pain causes you to drop the rod, and it falls to the ground. The wolf snarls at you, and then it bolts after an old ewe.

You've chased off many wolves before, but you are in too much pain to do it now. You can't think straight. You decide to go find help. You ignore the urgent bleats of your frightened sheep. Passing the carcass of a dead lamb, you start for home.

You hear Reuben calling from the other side of the pasture. "Use your sling!"

You think there might be more than one wolf. Your mind is confused by the pain you are feeling. You can't find your sling. Reuben needs more help than what you can give him.

"I'm going for Father," you shout.

By the time your father reaches the flock, four sheep have been killed. Only later do you realize your mistake. You quit instead of staying to help Reuben any way you could. You feel awful.

By the next day, the whole town is talking about you. They laugh when Joash tells them how you bragged about fighting off enemy troops. He says, "The braggart couldn't even chase away an old wolf with one eye and three legs."

Joash is lying about the wolf, which had all its parts, but you hang your head anyway. Everyone thinks you are a coward. Cowards can't be soldiers. You give up on your dream of ever helping to save Judah from the enemy. You remain a shepherd for the rest of your life.

THE END

You see your rod on the ground not far away. You keep eye contact with the wolf as you edge closer to it. The wolf snarls, as if ready to pounce. Its coarse, gray hide bristles as it creeps closer. The sheep are bleating and bumping into each other.

Your rod is almost within reach. You pray that Reuben will arrive soon.

You lunge for your rod and then roll toward the beast. Swinging it across the ground, you trip the wolf. It lets out a whimper. You spring to your feet and ignore the pain of your throbbing ankle. Before the wolf can recover, you land a solid blow to its head. It goes limp, but you hit it again and again.

You hear Reuben's voice behind you. "I think it's dead." You stop hitting the beast but keep your rod poised in case it moves.

When it does not move, you throw your rod away from you. "It was attacking the sheep."

Reuben smiles. "You were unbelievable! That animal has terrorized the flocks around here for days. This will make you a hero."

A man you do not know is standing a few feet behind Reuben. Did he see everything? You feel blood rising to your face and give Reuben a questioning look.

"This is Simeon. I met him on the way here. He's got a message from the king for our town. I thought you could take him to see the elders."

"Sure," you say. Suddenly your foot gives out, and you drop to the ground.

"You're hurt," Reuben says.

"A little."

Reuben and Simeon wrap your foot with cloth while you tell them about Joash and your kinnor. You tie the kinnor to your chest.

"You've had quite a day," Simeon says. "Why don't you lean on me?" He puts an arm around your waist. You begin hobbling toward the village.

"What does King Jehoshaphat want to say to us?" you ask.

"Everyone must go to Jerusalem, because our enemies are about to attack," Simeon says. "Here, lean this way. It might be easier."

So the rumors are true. The little bumps and gullies on the path feel a lot deeper now.

Simeon continues, "Reuben tells me that you sing and play the kinnor. I'd love to hear it."

You smile but do not answer. It is one thing to sing for God and the sheep. The thought of singing for a stranger, especially a king's messenger, makes you tremble. You pretend to concentrate on walking. Simeon seems to understand and remains quiet. When you get to your house, he tells your parents about the king's message.

"You must stay with us," your mother says.

"Thank you for your hospitality," Simeon replies with a smile.

It would be hard for any visitor to turn down your mother's invitation, especially with the smell of fresh bread in the air.

After supper, Simeon asks again, "Would you play the kinnor and let me hear you sing?"

You are tired, and your ankle is throbbing. You really do not feel like singing.

CHOICE ONE: If you sing for Simeon, go to page 200.

CHOICE TWO: If you do not sing, go to page 201.

You head for Jerusalem. Although you don't know the exact route, you know the general direction. You travel as quickly as you can.

As you near Jerusalem, you are surprised at how many people are in the city. You even see friends from your village, and you find your parents.

"I am so sorry for running away," you tell them as they hug you.

"We should have believed you," they say. They hand you the kinnor. "When you left, Joash told the truth and brought this back."

You go to see the king. When you report to the king's ministers what you have seen and heard, you are surprised to learn that God has already spoken to the king about the foreign armies. Again, you are amazed at God's lovingkindness. As you are leaving the palace, you can't help but break out in song.

The next morning, a messenger from King Jehoshaphat wakes your family. "Please forgive the early hour," he says, "but the king has heard your child singing." He turns to you. "The king wants to reward your courage by having you join the Temple singers as they lead the army into battle today."

You smile. "I would like that. Where do I go?"

In the pale light of dawn, the servant leads you through the streets to the front of the ranks. Instead of soldiers, musicians are leading the way. You recognize some of them as Korahites and Kohathites, Temple singers like your great-grandfather, who played your kinnor decades before you. As the march to battle begins, you are in awe of the other singers. You realize what an honor it is to serve God as a musician. You discover that there are many ways to fight for Judah.

One of the best ways is to worship God in song. You march boldly forward as a warrior, a singing warrior.

God has already done many miraculous things for you and for your country. You can't wait to see His awesome power at work today.

THE END

You walk toward your village, or where you think your village might be, since you are not sure where you are. Because of the number of times that you lose your way, it takes you an entire day to reach home.

The village looks strange when you first walk into it. There are no people outside of their homes, no animal noises, no laughter. The streets are deserted. Even the herds are gone.

You hurry to your house. No one is home. It appears as though everyone left in a hurry. You do not know what to do.

You scrounge around for some food to make a meal for yourself and fall asleep on your bed. Over the next few days, you spend most of the time eating and sleeping. You become bored.

One day, two enemy soldiers come to town. They recognize you as the crazy child who visited their camp, and they start laughing again. They leave you alone. They do not stay long. You go from one house to the next and try to take care of things that your neighbors aren't there to do.

Finally after days and days, your family returns. You are overjoyed to see them, and they are thrilled to see you. Joash has told the truth and returned the kinnor to your father.

As you sit down to the first decent meal in days, your family tells you about how Judah is no longer threatened by foreigners. You are amazed. You tell them about your time in the enemies' camp and about what happened there. They laugh at your story. You can see that they do not believe you, not completely. But you don't care. You know the truth, and it does not matter what other people think of you anymore. God cares for you. He proved it by saving you from enemy soldiers—twice! That is enough for you.

THE END

◆ ◆ ◆

You enter the cave on the left and move forward cautiously. Something flies over your head and disappears outside. You hear other movement and wonder what kinds of creatures live in the cave. You hear a high-pitched whistle, and your lamp blows out.

Shaking, you tell yourself that the wind can't hurt you. And all those other sounds you hear are just your imagination. You run your hands along the cave's wall to find your way and continue down the passage.

Just as you are about ready to give up, your hand catches a sticky spiderweb. You try to shake it loose, which causes you to trip and fall into something slimy. Your elbow hits a sharp stone.

"Ouch! That Joash! I'll get him yet!" you yell to boost your courage. As you pull yourself up, your hand touches a smooth object. You touch it again and hear the faint sound of musical strings vibrating.

"I found it!" you say. You can't believe it. You hug the kinnor to your body and retrace your steps back to the cave entrance and then home.

In the morning, you show your parents the kinnor.

"I'm glad you found it," your father says. "Please be more careful from now on."

Your mother notices a few new scratches on the instrument.

The scratches look more like grooves to you. You can feel your anger rising. You want to get back at Joash for hurting your instrument. You know you are too small to fight him. You would not stand a chance.

Later, you take the kinnor to your secret place outside the village.

You sit down inside a group of large stones where no one can see or hear you. There you pour out your frustration to God in song, just as King David did. When you go back to the village, you find out that King Jehoshaphat has called all of Judah to Jerusalem. Enemies will attack soon.

Your whole village packs up and heads for Jerusalem. You take your kinnor on the journey. That evening, you sing for the people to keep up spirits and quiet fears. Soon other townspeople sing with you, even Joash. You do not mind. You, Joash, and all the rest of the people are in this together.

THE END

You climb down into the cave on your right. You do not have to wait long for your eyes to get used to the darkness, since you came into it from the night. The lamp lights your way. You hold it out in front of you and search every crevice for your kinnor.

After some time, the cave narrows down to nothing. You have searched most of the night and have not found what you came for. You return home. If you get a good night's rest, perhaps you can go back tomorrow night to search the other cave. You lie down on your mat, exhausted.

All too soon, your mother is shaking you. "Wake up! We have to pack."

King Jehoshaphat has sent messengers all over Judah. Everyone has to meet with him in Jerusalem.

You do not want your kinnor to wait in a cave until you return. The dampness will ruin it, but you can't go looking for it until you get back. You are so angry with Joash that you find him on the streets of your village.

"You traitor! You Ammonite!" You push his shoulder as hard as you can and then hit him.

Joash is surprised by your attack. You have never had the nerve to fight him before. You lunge at him again before he can say anything. Your anger makes you stronger. And without his buddies, Joash does not seem so powerful.

Within moments, though, he gets angry and starts fighting back. He punches you, and your stomach feels as if it has been pushed up to your throat. As you wrestle to the ground, you hear your tunic ripping.

"Stop this, both of you!" You feel strong arms pulling you and Joash apart.

"I didn't start it," complains Joash. You are surprised at how small he looks next to his father.

"People of Judah should live together in peace," his father says. "We'll be fighting foreigners soon enough. Come, Son. We have to get ready to leave." Joash glances back at you as they walk away. He does not look as mean as before.

You walk home. You feel bile rise to your mouth from your stomach and can't seem to get rid of that bitter taste. You feel as though you could throw up.

Your father meets you at the door. "Why aren't you packing?" he says. "You should be getting ready to leave." You know he is distracted, because he does not notice your torn tunic.

"I'm sorry," you say. Joash's father's words trouble you. You ask, "Are we really going to have a war?"

"Yes." He hurries away to prepare so that you can leave immediately. You help your mother and brother pack.

Later, Joash comes to your house. "Here." He thrusts your kinnor at you and then disappears. You think it might be his way of apologizing.

"I'm sorry too!" you call after him.

As you close the door, you remember what his father said: "People of Judah should live together in peace." You decide that if you get through this war alive, you will try to make friends with Joash.

THE END

◆ ◆ ◆

When your family starts to leave, you tell your father, "Someone should guard the village."

He shakes his head no. "The king has summoned us. We need to obey. God will watch over our town."

You know you should listen to your father, but hiding in Jerusalem is for cowards, not for heroes. As the whole town heads toward Jerusalem, you slip farther and farther behind until you reach the end of the group. You dart behind a boulder and hide until the bleating of sheep and barking of dogs have faded away.

You are glad you planned ahead and brought your scrip. You fill it with smooth stones for the battle you expect to come. The only sound you hear is the scraping of your leather sandals on the dirt road. The cloud-filled sky seems to grow angry, and the rock-speckled hills lose their friendliness. Maybe you can catch up with the others. You turn around to run after them, but then you remember Joash's taunting. He would call you a coward. You continue toward the village.

The deserted town has taken on a new darkness. You had no idea that silence could beat so loudly against your ears. You scrounge for food. Everything you find is cold and tastes moldy. You curl up on your mat. It feels even harder than usual as you wait for daybreak with your rod at your side.

The next morning is sunny, and you set up a watch just outside of town. It feels odd to be on watch without the sheep. All the animals are with your family. The days seem longer now, especially because you can't sing to pass the time. That would give away your position.

You know you are drifting from God—you hardly even think of Him anymore—but you don't have the energy to bother about that. You have to take care of yourself.

One afternoon, you are sitting on a rock watching the horizon. Everything looks so wavy in the heat that it almost makes you dizzy. You lean over to get a drink of water from the animal skin in the shade by your feet. Suddenly two strong arms grab you from behind. They feel like iron bands around your chest. You try to wrestle free, but soon find yourself on the ground with a knife pressed against your throat. Angry, dark eyes stare into yours. You realize that your assailant is an Ammonite spy. You wonder how he was able to get past your watch.

"Where are the people of this town?" he demands.

"What town?" you say.

He kills you for being a smart aleck.

THE END

You leave with your family for Jerusalem. Your ankle heals fairly quickly, since it was just a slight sprain. Your family is traveling with others from your village for protection from bandits and wild animals. You try to avoid Joash and his friends, but you have to help keep your family's sheep moving in the right direction. Sometimes the bullies fall back to where you are just to taunt you.

You arrive at Jerusalem without incident, and the king has called a fast for all of Judah. You hate going hungry, but Judah needs God's help. People from all the towns have come to fast and pray. From what you have heard, only a miracle can save your country now.

Simeon finds your family at the camp your town has set up inside the city walls. You welcome him into your tent as a friend but are surprised at his words.

"I'd like you to sing for my master, one of the Temple singers."

When Simeon tells you the man's name, your mother says, "He's a distant cousin. Like you, he is a Kohathite descendant of Levi."

You are not sure what to say.

"It would be an honor to sing for this man," your father says. It was his gentle way of telling you that you should go with Simeon. All you can think about is your growling stomach. You feel a little faint.

"Your music gave me such peace from God," Simeon says. "Won't you please allow my master that same peace?"

"I think you should do it," your mother says. "But it's your choice."

CHOICE ONE: If you sing for Simeon's master,
go to page 231.

CHOICE TWO: If you do not sing for Simeon's master,
go to page 233.

"I was kicked out," you say and try to look as dejected as possible. "No one in Judah wants me around."

"Why did you run from us then?" asks a man.

"I run from everyone," you say. "I am not liked by others." You know you are lying, but you think the man believes you. "I am an orphan. No one wanted another mouth to feed. I have lived on my own in the wilderness for many years."

The man talks quietly to the others. You know you look disheveled. You think they are discussing whether or not your story is true, but they are talking so fast that you can understand only a few words. You try not to act as though you are interested.

Finally, the man says, "Come with me." You follow him, not knowing if they believed you or not.

You walk through the entire camp, and it takes a long time. There are thousands of soldiers. You wonder if Judah has any chance at all against so many. You pass tent after tent and see swords and spears everywhere.

At the end of the camp is a caravan.

"You are now my slave, the slave of Hazzan," the soldier says. He gives instructions to the caravan. You are chained to a camel. You walk for days. Finally, when you think your legs can't move another step, you reach a large house. It is your new master's house, Hazzan's house.

You do not get to sleep in the big house, but in the stable. It smells of animal waste. Your job is to feed and care for the pigs. You get to eat whatever slop they leave, and that isn't much. After all, they eat like pigs. You grow used to the fermented, mildewed, and muddy tastes of your meals. You wait for your master to return, but he never does. You wonder why.

THE END

◆ ◆ ◆

You know that they won't believe you, but you tell your whole story anyway. You tell how Joash stole your kinnor and then lied about it. You tell how your parents reacted, and how hurt that made you feel.

"I ran away. I ran most of the night." While you are speaking, you are sorry for not waiting at home for the truth to come out. It usually does. You know your parents love you, and you wish you had never left.

Knowing that this is probably the last time that you will be given a chance to speak before they kill you, you decide to tell the enemy soldiers what you really think of them.

You say, "The God of Judah is all powerful, mightier than you and all of your false gods put together. You can't hurt me unless my God lets you. If He wanted to, He could help me fight all of you at once, and I would win."

The men throw back their heads and roar with laughter. You stand proudly waiting for death, but no one takes you seriously. They think you are crazy. They give you lukewarm water and stale bread, and then they let you go.

As you stand outside the foreigners' camp, you thank God for saving your life. It astonishes you that He would care for you even after you ran away in anger.

CHOICE ONE: If you head for Jerusalem to warn King Jehoshaphat about the enemy army, go to page 213.

CHOICE TWO: If you head back to your village, go to page 215.

◆ ◆ ◆

You nod and follow him. The slave leads you around the back part of the camp and into a small tent.

"This is where I stay," he says. "You will be safe here until dark."

"Why are you helping me?" you ask.

"I have been a slave all of my life," he says. "If they find you, they will make you a slave too. I would not wish my hard life on anyone."

You nod. "Thank you."

"There's food over there," he says before he disappears.

You wait in the small tent alone. You try to stay alert in case of trouble, but your long run yesterday wore you out. By afternoon, you fall asleep.

Just before dawn of the next day, the slave wakes you.

"It is time," he says. You follow him out of the tent and to the edge of the camp. He leads you to a path that is barely visible in the early morning light.

Just after you pass some large rocks, two men who smell like camel dung grab you. They hold your wrists together in a tight grasp.

"This is the spy," the boy says. "I want my silver."

"What are you doing?" you yell.

A hand comes over your mouth and presses in until you taste filth. Now you are sure the smell was camel dung. You gag and want to spit the horrible flavor out.

"If you make another sound," says a rough voice, "I won't be so nice." You are really scared.

Someone tosses the slave a coin. "Now get out of here before I decide to take you with me as a slave too."

"Humph," says the slave. He turns to you. "It isn't personal. With this money, I can buy my freedom. Anyway, being a slave is better than being dead. I saved your life." He turns and leaves. The men carry you to the other side of the ridge. Waiting for them is a small caravan.

You travel to Egypt and live there as a slave for the rest of your life.

THE END

◆ ◆ ◆

Y ou don't trust the boy, but you nod. He moves away from you, and you follow. As soon as you have your footing and his back is turned, you break into a run.

Within seconds, you hear him shouting, "Enemy spy! Enemy spy!" Almost immediately, you hear the thud of feet running behind you. They are gaining on you, but you do not look back.

Vice-like hands grab you from behind. They jerk you to a halt. You are out of breath and coughing. They half-carry and half-drag you back to their camp.

You are thrown on the ground in front of a high-ranking soldier. He pulls you by your hair to a kneeling position and makes you face him. He smells like strange spices, but they don't cover up the fact that he probably has not had a bath in years. You wish he would move one step away from you.

"You seem too young to be a spy. Are you the best that Judah can do?"

CHOICE ONE: If you tell him that you are an outcast from Judah, go to page 224.

CHOICE TWO: If you tell him that you ran away from your parents, go to page 226.

You nod. You can't even find your voice to agree. You almost wish that you had never played for Simeon in the first place.

That evening, you are brought to the outer courtyard of the great Temple to sing before Simeon's master. Before you begin, you wipe your hands on your tunic and wonder how cold hands can sweat. You tremble as you hold the kinnor and position your fingers over the strings. Simeon's master smiles to encourage you. You are afraid to look at him, so you close your eyes and try to sing just to God. The distant smell of incense helps remind you that God is near. You sing of God's victory against the Egyptians.

As you finish, you notice that the courtyard is silent. You open your eyes to see why. A man is watching you. Everyone else is bowing. It's King Jehoshaphat! You stand up and bow, too, almost dropping the kinnor. When you look up again, the king is gone.

"Thank you," Simeon's master says. He gives you a cool drink of water. You feel it hit the bottom of your empty stomach. All the people are gathering outside of the Temple to hear King Jehoshaphat.

"Stay with me," Simeon says, "so you won't get lost in this crowd." You tie your kinnor around your waist and keep close to him.

All of Judah is there when Jehoshaphat stands up to speak. Instead of giving a speech he prays, "O Lord, God of our fathers, are You not the God who is in heaven? You rule over all the kingdoms of the nations. Power and might are in Your hand, and no one can withstand You."

The king prays a long time. He finishes with, "O our God, will You not judge them? For we have no power to face this vast army that is attacking us. We do not know what to do, but our eyes are upon You."

All the people pray with him, but silently. You had no idea that the enemy was so strong. Even the king is afraid. A man stands up suddenly. Simeon tells you that his name is Jahaziel.

"Listen, King Jehoshaphat and all who live in Judah and Jerusalem!" he says. This is what the Lord says to you: 'Do not be afraid or discouraged because of this vast army. For the battle is not yours, but God's. . . .'"

When he finishes speaking, Jehoshaphat bows down to worship the Lord with his face to the ground. Everyone else does the same, including you. Suddenly, some Levites stand up and start shouting, praising God as loudly as they can. You feel God's power and can't help but stand up and join in, waving your arms in the air.

You wake up early the next morning, anxious for God's battle to begin. As the soldiers are about to leave, Jehoshaphat decides to have singers lead the way, praising the great and holy Lord. You are standing with Simeon as his master is chosen.

"And you will sing, too," King Jehoshaphat says. You look up to see him pointing right at you! You smile in acknowledgement of his words. You are overjoyed as the king leaves.

Someone sidles up to you and whispers in your ear. "Better you than me." It is Joash.

"What do you mean? It's a great honor."

"No, I'd call it a great strategy. The king knows that the enemy will be tired of killing singers before they ever get to the soldiers. It will give Judah the advantage."

Joash gives you a tight hug. He appears sincere when he says, "Thank you for sacrificing yourself for the good of your people."

Before you can answer, he walks away.

CHOICE ONE: If you join the singers, go to page 207.

**CHOICE TWO: If you do not join the singers,
go to page 208.**

You think about singing in public. What if the soldiers heard you? You would look like a sissy to the bravest men of Judah.

"Thank you, Simeon," you say, "but I would rather wait until I can eat again. I don't want the rumblings of my stomach to drown out my singing." Everyone laughs.

"Perhaps you can train your stomach to keep time to the music," Reuben says.

Simeon is gracious. "My master would appreciate hearing you whenever you're ready. Thank you."

You feel bad about turning Simeon down, so you offer to walk partway home with him. The crowded city teems with voices. The odor of animal dung stings your nostrils. You hear some loud praying. Through open tent flaps, you hear children whining for food in chorus with the bleating of sheep and goats in their makeshift pens. You notice that a large group of soldiers have camped together. You stop. Simeon sees your interest and suggests that you visit. He introduces you to a guard before he leaves.

"Interested in soldiering, are you?" the guard asks, chuckling. "Go ahead and take a look around."

As you pick your way through the area, some soldiers smile at you. Many are praying and do not notice you at all. Others stare into space. You wonder if soldiers get just as scared as everyone else. Two soldiers are talking by an unlit fire pit. You join them.

"Can you believe it?" the older soldier says. "Isaac, my arms bearer, is sick. I don't think he'll be able to march into battle with us."

"You'll have to carry all your weapons yourself," another says. He has a scar on his cheek.

Your ears perk up. Maybe you could be the man's arms bearer for the battle! "Excuse me, but I would be happy to help," you say. "I know I'm small, but I'm strong. And I'm a deadeye with a sling."

The men appear amused, as if they think you are joking. Finally, the man with the scar puts his face right up to yours. "Prove it."

You never go anywhere without your sling, so you pull it from the girdle tied around your waist.

"See that jar over there?" You point to an earthenware jar at the far side of the camp. You load a smooth stone into the sling, swing, aim, and fire. The jar shatters.

"You have a job." The older man said. "My name is Enan. When the time comes, you will march into battle at my side."

When you tell your parents, your mother looks worried. Your father says, "Maybe this will help you get this idea of soldiering out of your system. Do what you're asked to do and you'll be fine."

Your mother harrumphs. "I'll be praying that Isaac has a miraculous recovery."

The day arrives for the soldiers to leave. As you march in the midst of Judah's army, you feel like an ant in tall grass. The soldiers look so fierce! It takes all your courage just to stay with them. You are near the back of the column of soldiers. Then after all of your walking, Enan does not even get to the battle before it is over. You are not sure who was killed or who fought, but you help him pick up the spoils from the enemy.

When you return to Jerusalem, Enan gives you some of the spoils—the things you took from the enemy camp—to bring to your parents. Your family is thankful for the many fine things that you bring to them. Enan's arms bearer is well again, so you help your parents get ready for the trip home.

THE END

Y ou don't want to be responsible for losing your family's kinnor. You decide never to play it around Joash again. When Reuben relieves you, you hurry home to have a good cry.

Your father greets you at the door. "Hurry to the rabbi's house with your kinnor. A king's messenger has arrived. I volunteered you to sing for him. Gideon's sending his son over too."

"You mean Joash?"

Your father nods. When you arrive, Joash looks as upset as you feel. You try to hide your kinnor behind a leg of the rabbi's table.

"Boys, why don't you sing King David's first psalm?" the rabbi asks. You begin. You are amazed at how well your voices blend together.

When you are done, the messenger says, "Excellent! Would you sing again and play your kinnor this time?"

You steal a glance at Joash. He looks from you to the messenger. Without a word, he brings your instrument to you.

"Thanks," you say. You both smile. From that day forward you live together in perfect harmony.

THE END

You become angrier and angrier about Joash's bullying. For the rest of the day, you try to think of a way to make Joash pay for what he did to you. You hide behind a rock near his house, waiting for your opportunity.

"Joash," his mother calls, "I'm leaving the soup on the fire. Stay here and watch it until I get back. Stir it every few minutes so it won't burn."

"Sure," says Joash, but as soon as his mother is out of sight, he pulls the pot away from the fire and runs to his friend's house. Quickly, you grab two handfuls of dirt, dump them into the soup, and push the pot over the highest flames. You run back to your hiding place. Joash returns and stares at the pot, confused. His mother walks in just as he starts stirring.

She takes one look at the soup and begins to shriek. "It's burnt!" She tastes it and spits out the food into a cloth. "What have you done? You have ruined our evening meal." She grabs him by the ear. "This is the last prank you will ever pull."

Joash looks dumbfounded. "But I did what you said."

You smile. If he admits to leaving, he will get in trouble for disobeying. If he says he stayed, he will be blamed for the spoiled soup. Your job is done. *It serves him right*, you think.

Soon your gloating is swept aside when you hear the report from a messenger. "King Jehoshaphat is calling all of Judah to Jerusalem."

After the announcement, your family hurries home to pack. You find your broken staff just outside the door.

How did Joash know I did it? you wonder. As you tie bundles of clothes and food, you plan how to get even with Joash for breaking your staff.

That is how your life goes from then on. You and Joash keep harming each other. Nothing is as important to you as being one-up on Joash. You lead a miserable life.

THE END

◆ ◆ ◆

You quickly close the tent flap and try to hide under the covering you used the night before. The noise and killing continue outside. There seems to be no end to it. You try to eat the leftover bread from your master's breakfast, but it tastes stale.

Suddenly your master stumbles into the tent. He has been stabbed. You try to stay hidden, but he sees you.

"Come here, child," he says.

Perhaps he will give you your freedom now. Cautiously, you inch toward him, keeping the doorway in view. Blood is pouring from his wound.

"I am dying," he says.

You can't help but ask, "Now do you believe in the power of Judah's God?"

"Judah's God? What has your God to do with it?"

You think his answer is odd.

He grabs your arm with a bloody hand. "If I have to die, so do you." Before you can get away, he stabs you. You die on the floor of the tent beside him.

THE END

You shut the goat-hair flap and pray for courage. Then you hurry to the shaded side of the tent. You have been working a section of it loose for days, every moment that you were left alone. You lift up the bottom edge and slide underneath it, scraping against the ground as you do it. You are outside.

Shadows are still deep on this side of the tent. You silently race from the shadow of one tent to the shadow of the next tent. Several times you must wait for fighting to stop and your escape route to clear.

Sometimes you have to scurry over fallen bodies to reach the next shadow. Three tents left to pass. Two tents. One tent. As soon as you pass the last tent, you are in sunlight. You enjoy the warmth of it on your face.

You take off at a run, hoping that the soldiers are too busy fighting to notice you. The noise of battle, metal on metal, and the groans of the dying fade behind you. You press on, ignoring the sharp rocks cutting into your feet through the holes in your sandals.

You reach a small rise of ground with a protective rock outcropping. You slide behind the rocks and hold your stomach to catch your breath.

From your vantage point, you can see the whole camp. It is strewn with bodies. Where is Judah? King Jehoshaphat's soldiers are not even there! The Ammonites and Moabites have killed all the men from Mount Seir. Now they are killing each other!

"This has to be the work of God," you say out loud. "God made Judah's enemies turn on themselves!"

Before too long, all is silent. The breeze no longer brings you the occasional sound of dying men. Your mouth is dry, but you don't leave the rocks to find water. In the distance, you hear a loud, musical sound. Who could it be? Now you can see an army marching toward the foreigners' camp.

You listen closely. The noise is music. You recognize the words. You recognize Judah's army.

Judah is singing praises to God!

You shake your head. Your God is even more amazing than you thought. You raise your voice and worship God in song.

THE END

Escape!

Escape!

"Come on!" Beker shouts. Beker is the best thief in all of Jerusalem. No one has ever seen her long, slender fingers steal a single coin.

"This crowd is enormous," Mahol says. "We're going to eat well tonight." Mahol is the brains of your group. He is tall and can talk his way out of almost anything. He continues, "Now's our chance to lighten a few purses."

You have survived because you run fast.

Ever since you can remember, you have been an orphan. You and dozens of other orphans live on the streets of Jerusalem. You steal together and do whatever is necessary to survive.

Mahol, Beker, and you work your way down the street. When you get near the crowd, you split up and blend in. The sweat of so many people all in one place fills the air around you. The people are shouting, "Hosanna! Blessed is he who comes in the name of the Lord."

They are shouting to a man riding a donkey. Some people are calling him a king, but he looks poor to you. You are about to steal a stout man's coins from a soft pouch when you hear someone say, "Jesus healed me from being blind. Hosanna!" You look. The man next to you is blind Matthias, but now he can see. How can that be?

You have heard of this Jesus. You heard that He did many miracles—healed diseases and fed thousands of people with only a little food. Some say He even brought a dead man back to life. Perhaps they will crown Him king.

You push through the crowd to see Him better. He looks straight at you. His eyes are gentle, and it feels as if He knows you. You shake your head. You have never seen Him before in your life.

"He is the Messiah! Hosanna!" shouts a woman. You look at the ground. You don't want to steal from this crowd. Later that night, Mahol shares a piece of bread with you so you do not go hungry.

A few days later Beker tells you, "Do you remember that Jesus fellow we saw on the donkey?" You nod, and she continues, "He was arrested."

"By Rome?" you ask.

She shakes her head. "No, the Council."

The next day, the streets are clogged with people. You hear women weeping. The crowd parts for Roman soldiers. You can tell by the nails one soldier is carrying that there is to be a crucifixion, but why are they using nails today? Sometimes they use only ropes. The criminal being crucified must have done something terribly wrong. You shudder at the thought of people dying so cruelly. It has always been one of your biggest fears that you might be caught and then crucified. Crucifixion is too horrible to watch.

You start to leave, but then you hear someone cry out, "Jesus!" You look at the man who has just fallen under a cross. His face is torn and bleeding. How can anyone tell who He is? He looks at you, and you recognize the kindness in His eyes. You let the crowd push you toward Golgotha, where Jesus is nailed to the cross beside two other crucified men. Somehow you just cannot bring yourself to steal from anyone today.

After a few days, you are stealing for your daily bread again. One day, after an especially big heist, Beker says, "Did you hear the latest? People are saying that Jesus rose from the dead."

"Yeah, right," you say.

Beker laughs.

It has been weeks since you heard the resurrection rumors. Today a lot of foreigners are in Jerusalem. You walk toward a noisy crowd listening to some men talk.

Your friend Mahol says, "Big crowds mean big pickings."

"I wonder what's going on," you say.

"Who cares?" Mahol answers and moves into the midst of the crowd, on the lookout for easy coins.

When he is gone, a woman turns to you. "Those men are Jesus' disciples. Everyone listening is hearing them in their own language."

You give her a strange look.

"I know it doesn't make sense," she says, "but it's true. The one speaking over there is named Peter." You edge closer to listen. Peter talks about Jesus. What Peter says makes sense to you—the kindness in Jesus' eyes, His death, and His resurrection.

CHOICE ONE: If you find yourself believing in Jesus as God, go to page 246.

CHOICE TWO: If you go back to stealing, go to page 248.

◆ ◆ ◆

No lightning struck, but you suddenly know that you are changed in some huge way.

The woman who spoke to you earlier puts a hand on your shoulder. "Why don't you come over for dinner?" she says.

You eat dinner with Anna, her husband, Joshua, and their two girls. You end up staying with them for several weeks, becoming a welcome part of their family. You begin to understand Jesus' love even more through them. Now you are one of Jesus' followers too.

Today you are helping Stephen, another follower of Jesus, get food ready for some widows. You watch him work. Stephen is not afraid of anyone. He speaks boldly about Jesus and has done many miracles in Jesus' name. You hope to be like Stephen someday.

"Make sure Hannah gets her bread," he says. He hands you two loaves of warm bread. You nod and tie them into your cloak.

Suddenly four guards walk to where Stephen is and grab him.

"What are you doing?" you ask. You are knocked to the side.

"Is the kid with him?" one of the guards asks. His voice is rough and without emotion.

As two guards drag Stephen away, the other two turn toward you. You dart through the crowd to escape. They follow you.

CHOICE ONE: If you lose the guards and then get to Hannah's, go to page 249.

CHOICE TWO: If you lose the guards and then decide never to go near those dangerous followers of Jesus again, go to page 253.

CHOICE THREE: If you lose the guards and then go for help, go to page 255.

◆ ◆ ◆

You ignore what Peter says and steal enough money for a great dinner. After a few more weeks of taking small money pouches, you break into a rich man's house. A bag of coins is lying beside the man's bed. You sneak into the room. The man's snores are steady. You creep up to where his hand rests beside his moneybag. As you reach for the bag, the man snorts and turns toward you. You dive behind a chair. Whew! He is still asleep. You return to his side, lift the bag, and quietly creep out of the room.

Setting the bag on the floor, you hike your leg over the windowsill. When you reach back for the bag, you find that it is heavier. You can't budge it. Suddenly a tingling feeling runs down your spine. The rich man is standing beside you. His foot is holding the bag.

You have visions of being crucified, but the man takes you into his house. His name is Joseph of Arimathea. He becomes your family and teaches you about Jesus. He takes you to see the empty tomb, the same tomb that he let Jesus use for His burial. Finally, you become a believer. You never steal again.

THE END

You dodge past people and into the maze of Jerusalem's streets, just like you used to do with Mahol and Beker. Left at the tax collector's stand. Right behind the potter's shed. Left through the alley behind Rabbi Levi's home. Two rights, and you scrape your back on a rock that juts out. You crawl through a hole into a deserted courtyard. You wait.

Footsteps hurry past your hiding place. You wait. They come back, slower this time. Not until they have walked past you a third time do you ease yourself out of the hole.

Quickly you make your way to Hannah's house. You knock on her door and untie the bread. Its fragrance leaps back into the air as if nothing had happened. She recognizes you from the gatherings of believers and lets you in.

"These are from Stephen," you tell her. "He's been arrested."

She nods sadly. "I'll pray for him."

"They were after me, too, but I got away. I'm going to go find out what has happened to Stephen."

"I'll pray for you, too," she says.

You race across the city and to the Temple. Just outside the doorway to the Sanhedrin, you see a young Temple guard who is a believer.

"What's happening in there?" you ask.

"They accused Stephen of speaking against the Temple and the Law."

"How can they say that?" you demand.

"They're all lies. But he stayed so calm. I saw his face glow like an angel. He's in there now talking about everything from Abraham to Jesus of Nazareth." You both stop to listen, but the voices sound muffled to you, and you can only understand an occasional word.

You hear an uproar from the Council Room. "What did Stephen say? What's going on? I couldn't hear."

Your friend stifles a smile. "He called the Council stiff-necked, uncircumcised, and murderers."

You shake your head. "They're not going to like that." You lean a hand against the smooth wall beside you. Suddenly the whole Council erupts with shouting. It sounds like dozens of two-year-olds throwing tantrums.

You edge closer and hear Stephen's voice over the crowd. "Look, I see heaven open and the Son of Man standing at the right hand of God." You and the guard look up, but you only see the sky.

Men suddenly burst out of the chamber. Your friend pulls you to the side. The faces of the Councilmen are bulging into deep red and purple colors.

"Blasphemer!" they shout. "Stone him!"

Stephen must be somewhere in the middle of those angry voices. You hurry to keep up with them. They are heading outside the city. They really are going to stone Stephen! You follow and then stand helplessly by as men lay their robes down at the feet of the man standing next to you. He's obviously a leader.

People pick up stones and start throwing them at Stephen. Big ones. Small ones. When they hit Stephen's body, you cringe. *Thunk! Thunk! Crack!* You wonder if Stephen's bones are breaking, yet Stephen's face is glowing. You wish there was a way for you to help him escape, but the rocks keep coming.

Someone comes over to talk to the man beside you. "Well, Saul," he says. "It's good to be rid of one blasphemer."

Saul smiles. "We're just getting started." A chill runs down your back. You have a bitter taste in your mouth. The rocks are flying faster and faster at Stephen. He cannot possibly survive.

Wait! Stephen is saying something. "Lord Jesus, receive my spirit."

He drops to his knees. "Lord, do not hold this sin against them." He slumps to the ground.

CHOICE ONE: If you scream, "No!" go to page 265.

CHOICE TWO: If you force yourself to keep quiet, go to page 302.

You hurry through the gates of Jerusalem and head for the hills nearby. You find a cave for shelter. Its coolness is refreshing. Sheep graze on a hillside not far away. After days in your new location, and when your stomach is so empty it hurts, you find their owner.

"I'd like to watch your sheep for you in return for food," you say.

The owner looks you over. "I had a good shepherd, but he was a follower of Jesus of Nazareth. He left when he heard that a man was stoned to death for believing."

Stoned to death? Could he mean Stephen? The news shocks you, but you do not let the man know. It could be dangerous to tell him that you also are a follower of Jesus.

"How long would you stay?" the man asks.

"I'll stay as long as I can. Will you teach me how to care for your sheep?"

The man agrees. You live in a shepherd's hut and keep the sheep safe. You enjoy a bowl of lamb stew almost every day. When travelers pass by, which is not too often, you share what you have with them.

One day a man passes through the area. You recognize him as Palti, a follower of Jesus from Jerusalem. You give him food and a place to stay. He does not seem to recognize you.

"How did you get those bruises?" you ask.

"Saul and his men have gone crazy. They beat up the followers of Jesus and throw many of them into prison. They've even killed some. I'm headed elsewhere."

"I used to know a family who lived in Jerusalem," you say casually.

"The man's name was Joshua, and his wife's name was Anna. They were followers of Jesus. Did you know them?"

Palti shakes his head. "If they haven't left the city, then they are probably in prison—or dead."

Your heart feels heavy.

CHOICE ONE: If you leave with Palti when he goes, go to page 320.

CHOICE TWO: If you return to Jerusalem to find Joshua's family, go to page 268.

You hurry home and tell Joshua, "Stephen is in trouble. They've arrested him. What should we do?"

"I don't know," Joshua says. "We'll try to find one of the apostles. You check the marketplace, and I'll head toward the Temple."

You agree and take off running. Peter and John are always preaching somewhere. They should be easy to find. You run throughout Jerusalem all morning. Today, you cannot find them anywhere.

When you arrive home, Joshua has already returned. "I couldn't find anyone," you say.

In a serious voice, Joshua says, "Sit down." You sit on a stool.

"What happened?"

"Stephen is dead," Joshua says.

Your mind feels jumbled and confused. "What? But I was with him just a little while ago. There has to be some mistake!"

"He was stoned to death," Anna says.

"Stoned to death? Why? He didn't do anything wrong." You run your fingers through your hair. This cannot be happening.

"Stephen was condemned for blasphemy against God, the Law of Moses, and the Temple," Joshua says.

"But Stephen never showed any disrespect for God or holy things."

"In the eyes of the Council, it is wrong to believe that Jesus is the Son of God."

"Then that makes everyone who believes in Jesus a criminal." A new kind of fear fills your heart. "If they killed Stephen, then what will keep them from killing us, too?"

"Nothing," Anna says.

"We're thinking about moving," says Joshua.

You look at Rachel playing on the floor and Naomi cuddling her doll. Then you agree. "It's our only option."

Joshua rubs his beard. "You know the guards at the gates and how they do things. Should we leave immediately or wait until tonight?"

CHOICE ONE: If you advise the family to leave tonight, go to page 291.

CHOICE TWO: If you urge the family to pack and leave immediately, go to page 310.

Although you feel awful for Simeon, your family is counting on you. They must come first. You climb to the rooftop and put the ropes in place. You scout out possible avenues of escape. When your family arrives, everything is ready. They are somber. Even little Rachel is silent. Your heart aches for how much they must give up as they leave Jerusalem.

"The children first," Joshua whispers. You nod. Together, you lower Naomi.

Before you lower Rachel, she leans forward and gives you a hug. "I love you." You kiss her soft cheek and then lower her to where Naomi is waiting. Without another word, you work to get Anna over the wall and safely down to her children.

You and Joshua use both ropes to lower the family's possessions—but then you hear a noise. Soldiers are marching nearby. You both duck into the hay where you have been standing. It smells moldy, as if it needs to be tossed out. You wait for the soldiers to pass. It seems to take ages. There is time to look up into the heavens at the stars blinking through the darkened night. You are amazed at God's handiwork.

Joshua nudges you. "They're gone. We'd better hurry before the tenants come up to stargaze or get rainwater to drink."

You give him a smile. "I know we should be terrified by all of this, but somehow when I know God is with us, nothing seems quite as bad."

Joshua pats your back. "You go next."

"No," you say. "I know how to climb down the wall without a rope. Besides, if I don't make it, you can still take care of the family. Think of them."

"God has done such a work in your heart," Joshua says.

Slowly you let Joshua down. Just as he reaches the ground, you hear the sound of footsteps. Someone is on the roof. Quickly you untie the rope so that it falls to the ground next to Joshua. You know he will understand. You dart under the hay again. A second coil of rope is lying on the roof not far from where you are hiding. You forgot to kick it under the hay. You hold your breath.

The newcomer is a man. He paces back and forth on his rooftop as if he is in deep thought. In his wanderings, he eventually trips over the rolled rope.

"Where did this come from?" he says aloud. He picks it up, examines it, and then carries it back toward the steps to the house. You hear him say, "Martha, where did we get this rope?" The door shuts behind him.

You must leave quickly before he returns. You rush back to the wall and slowly slide over the top. You begin to climb down. One foot. One hand. One foot. One hand. You are only halfway down when it happens. Your foot slips and yanks your hand from its perch. You frantically grab for the wall, but your hand slices through the empty air. You feel yourself falling.

Your breath is knocked out of you when you land, but you do not feel any pain. You hear voices whispering around you. It takes a moment for you to realize that you did not hit the ground. You are in Joshua's arms. He caught you. You want to shout your thanks, but you know that you must be quiet. You give him a bear hug to show him how grateful you are.

You and your family escape without any other problems. You start a new life in another village. You tell everyone about Jesus and how He can change their lives, just as He did for you.

THE END

When Beker leaves, you find a merchant's cart, half-filled with hay, parked near you. You dive into the hay and hope that the merchant will be leaving Jerusalem soon. The hay is prickly against your skin, but you ignore it. You are extremely tired. You close your eyes.

When you wake up, the cart is moving. You peek out of the hay from the back of the wagon. It is night. You cannot tell where you are, but you know that you must be quite a distance from Jerusalem. It is dangerous to be alone at night, so you stay in the warm hay. The rocking motion of the cart lulls you back to sleep.

The next time you wake up, the cart has stopped. You cautiously slide yourself out of the wagon. It is parked in the back of a small farm. You shake the hay out of your hair, walk to the small house, and knock on the door. A woman with small eyes and a scowl on her mouth opens it.

You ask, "Do you have work I can do for food?" The smell of sweet bread greets you from the house.

The woman snorts. "Go away!"

"Who is it?" asks a friendly male voice.

"Another beggar."

"I'm looking for honest work," you call out to the man.

"A beggar?" He comes to the door. "You're just a child. Have you ever worked on a farm?"

You shake your head no but say, "I'm a good learner."

"This urchin is of no value to us," says the woman. "Children eat too much anyway."

"Children are a blessing from the Lord," the man says. He turns to you. "Why don't you go and fetch some water from the well." He points across the yard. "And then we'll talk."

You smile and run to the well. You'll never have to steal again.

THE END

◆ ◆ ◆

The next day, you and Mahol find a way to leave Jerusalem. Mahol shows you how to hide in a large earthenware jar and ride out of the city. Your legs cramp inside of the vessel as you bounce along. The inside of the jar is rough when you bump against it. The wagon keeps going for a very long time. When it stops, you find yourself in Bethlehem. By that time you can no longer feel your feet. You try to get out of the jar, but you have to move slowly. Your legs sting and tingle as the blood flows back into them. It takes a while before your legs feel normal.

Mahol glances around. "This looks just like Jerusalem." You eye him strangely. Bethlehem looks nothing like Jerusalem. Bethlehem's market is not as large, and the odor of animal droppings is barely noticeable. He sighs and sits down. "I guess this isn't the type of change that I was looking for."

Do you dare mention what you are thinking? Silently, you pray, "God, I need your help."

Out loud you say, "Maybe the change that you're looking for is on the inside."

He rolls his eyes. "You'd have to cut me open for a change like that."

"That's not what I meant. I'm a follower of Jesus, and He changed my heart."

Mahol does not look surprised. "I knew there was something different about you."

You tell him everything you learned from the apostles, Joshua, and Stephen. He asks all kinds of questions. Finally, Mahol accepts Jesus as his Messiah too.

You enjoy your time in Bethlehem together. During the day, you glean for grain on the edges of fields. You can chew on a handful of grain for quite a while. It seems like you always have food in your mouth. In the evening, you talk about God.

One day, Mahol grabs your arm. "We can't just stay here. We have to tell others about Jesus."

"Where do you want to go?" you ask.

"Back to Jerusalem. I want to tell all the other street kids about Jesus," he says.

CHOICE ONE: If you go with Mahol, go to page 309.

CHOICE TWO: If you leave to find your family,
go to page 298.

◆ ◆ ◆

Y ou lower your voice. "I am a follower of Jesus. They just killed a
believer named Stephen. I can't go home, because I don't want
anyone to follow me there. I'm willing to die for my beliefs, and I
know everyone in my family is too. But if I can keep them alive by
not going home, I will."

"I see," Mahol says. "I don't know about all this religious stuff,
but I'll tell your family to get out."

"Thank you," you say.

When Mahol leaves, you follow him at a distance. You weave
through the market stands filled with bread, duck, and fish so that
he does not know you are following him. You pray that you did not
make a mistake by telling him the truth. You do not want him to
report your family to the Council.

He heads toward your house. When he gets close to where your
family lives, you are satisfied. You lean against the rough walls of a
house and take a deep breath before you turn toward the gates of
Jerusalem. As you leave, no one seems to notice you.

You wait in the hills nearby for a few days, but you do not see
your family leave Jerusalem. Finally, you take the road to Samaria
and find work doing odd jobs for people. You are surprised at how
nice people are when you are helpful. You begin to make new friends.
They do not mind your talking about Jesus. Some of them even ask
you questions about Him.

A few months later, you are drawing water for a widow. You hear
a familiar voice say, "I'm thirsty." It is Rachel. You run over, pick her
up, and swing her around in a circle.

"I've found you!" you say. Still holding Rachel, you embrace Joshua, Anna, and Naomi.

"What about me?" It is Mahol's voice.

"Mahol?" You set Rachel down and give Mahol an enormous hug.

"What are you doing here?" you ask. Mahol looks unsure of himself. This surprises you.

Joshua laughs. "He came and told us what you said. Then he asked to know more about Jesus."

Mahol shrugs. "Since you thought He was worth dying for, I thought I ought to find out more about Him."

You give him another hug. "I am so glad. First you were my brother in the streets. Now you are my brother in Christ."

THE END

Yrou scream, "No!" You cannot believe that these angry men have killed your friend. You try to go to him, but the crowd is too thick and keeps you from moving forward.

A little voice in your head asks, "What if they stone you, too?" You have to get away.

You struggle free from the crowd. With tears in your eyes, you run back to the city, down the narrow streets to where your family lives. By the time you get there, you are sobbing. The taste of salt from your tears is on your tongue.

"They've killed him! They've killed Stephen!" Your family gathers around you—Rachel, Naomi, Joshua, and Anna. Anna puts her arms around you. She smells like the lentil soup that she has been making.

"Angry men drove Stephen from the city and stoned him to death," you tell them. A worried look passes between Anna and Joshua.

Joshua says, "It's only the beginning."

That night, you hear guards outside of your family's door. You peek through the window and notice Saul leading them. Did he follow you here?

CHOICE ONE: If you escape through a window,
go to page 278.

CHOICE TWO: If you fling the door open and fight,
go to page 295.

◆ ◆ ◆

You shout and pretend to stumble backward, toppling over the stand with birds and lambs. The squawking and commotion turn the guards' attention toward you. You grasp a handful of feathers to catch a fowl. Looking at the guards, you act as though you are going to steal it, then you drop it. Quickly you run away from the market, hoping you have given Joshua enough time to get through the gate.

You know the guards are chasing after you. Their footsteps pound in your ears as you dodge through streets and into alleys. You even go over two rooftops, but you cannot seem to lose them. Then you take a wrong turn, and you find yourself in a dead end. It will be only moments until the guards reach you. As you catch your breath, the animal odor on your clothes make you gag.

Then you see Mahol and Beker.

**CHOICE ONE: If you call to them for help,
go to page 290.**

CHOICE TWO: If you get out of the alley so that the guards do not grab your friends, go to page 311.

◆ ◆ ◆

You go to the owner of the sheep and tell him the truth. "I am a follower of Jesus. When we first met, I was running away from Jerusalem and those who wanted to kill me because of my new faith." You smell the lamb stew and know that you may never get another bowl of it.

Your boss nods. "I was praying for you. I did not know the source of your struggles, but I knew that you had many to face. Tell me about this Jesus whom you follow."

You tell him about Jesus' life, death, and resurrection.

"I always thought the Messiah would come as a mighty ruler," he says, "but the power Jesus showed was greater than any king's."

"So you believe that Jesus was raised from the dead and can forgive your sins?"

"Yes, I do. I know He is the Messiah, and I want to follow Him. Now if you'll excuse me, I want to pray about this."

"Welcome to God's family," you say with a smile. You go back to watching the sheep for the rest of the afternoon.

With your boss's blessing, you leave for Jerusalem the next day. Your stomach feels jittery, but God's peace settles on your heart as you enter the city gates. When you arrive at your family's house, you knock. Strangers answer the door.

"Do you know where Joshua and Anna went?" you ask.

"They were killed along with their children," the owners say. As you walk away from the house, sadness fills your heart. You wish you could have been with them at the end.

You can hear the squawking of birds from the market when a voice says, "Is that the one?"

"It is!" says a man who used to be your neighbor.

Guards roughly grab you. You do not try to resist. They bring you before the Council. Strangers come before the Council and say, "I heard this child speak against God and His holy Temple!"

"Listen," you say, "all I know is that Jesus saved me from my sin. He wants to save you, too. He's not dead anymore. He is the Messiah we've all been waiting for. He's the Son of the Living God."

"Blasphemer!" they shout. Your words have caused an uproar, but you barely hear the angry voices around you. Hands drag you out of the building, down the street, and out of Jerusalem. Peace, stronger than anything you have ever felt, washes over you. You pray for the people around you. If only they would come to know Jesus too.

When people begin throwing stones at you, they hurt, but not as much as you expected. You look up and see the kingdom of heaven opening before you. You are astounded at the beauty! And Jesus is there. This time He shines brighter than lightning. You would be frightened, but you see Him smiling at you. Kindness glows from His eyes.

You leave your body and fly straight into Jesus' arms.

THE END

◆ ◆ ◆

You whisper, "Go quickly."

Shomer nods and moves away with Maacah. You glance behind you. Maacah's hysterics are growing.

"Oh no! Soldiers! Run, Simeon!" you call as if Simeon is in the alley in front of you. You dart into the alley.

You can hear the soldiers yelling, "They went that way." As you round a corner, you smell horse droppings. You saw a man loading the dung into a cart earlier. The soldiers are gaining. You can hear the pounding of their feet.

You knock over a water jar and push a pile of the dung into the street where the soldiers will pass. Turning quickly, you climb the side of a building. You reach the top just as the soldiers reach the manure. They slip on it and fall down. When they regain their footing, they continue the chase, unaware that you are no longer in front of them.

You race across rooftops back to Simeon's house. You guide him to the escape wall. A rope is hanging over it. You smile. Your family must have gotten away safely! You and Simeon climb down. When your feet touch the ground, you laugh quietly. You have escaped! Although neither you nor Simeon is touching the rope, it moves. Someone is pulling on it!

"Thieves!" a man yells. "Help! Jerusalem is being attacked!" You and Simeon sprint away from the wall.

You trip on a ditch and hear, "Over there! Don't let them get away."

Simeon drops down beside you and motions for you to stay low. A cloud is about to cover the moon. When it does, you both run for another dip in the terrain. When the moon comes out, you see soldiers searching for you near the wall. You flatten yourselves against the hard dirt.

You point out a hill to Simeon. When another cloud covers the moon, you both run for it. From there, the soldiers do not find you.

Cautiously, you go to Bethlehem with Simeon.

Shomer tells you, "Your family is safe in Nazareth." You stay with Simeon until you hear a rumor that Saul has become a follower of Jesus. That disturbs you.

When you leave to find your family, you go to where Saul is first. Saul's other name is Paul, and now he is preaching about Jesus. You struggle with your feelings. This man killed Stephen. Then you remember your own sins.

You walk up to Paul and say, "Somehow Jesus forgave me. I'm going to have to forgive you."

"Thank you," Paul says. "God is amazing." His eyes are shining with such a love that you know without any doubt that Paul is your brother in Christ Jesus.

THE END

You do not answer him. You go to your family's home and help them pack. They take whatever they can carry.

"Where is your pack?" Joshua asks.

"I'm not going with you," you say.

"There's no future here," Joshua says.

You shrug. "Maybe not, but there are a lot of people who might need help."

Joshua nods. "That is very brave of you." You see him wavering, as if he would like to stay and help.

"You, on the other hand, have a family," you say.

Joshua smiles. "And I must take them to safety."

You both hug. Anna looks as if she will cry as she kisses you goodbye. You can smell a large pot of lentil soup that she has left behind for you.

When they leave, you are alone. You waste no time. You have been studying the prison for days. You follow Saul around town. The angry lines in his face tell you that he needs the peace you have found in the Lord. He does not see you as you slide in and out of alleys. Mahol and Beker see you, though. It feels good to be around your friends again. It is as if you never left.

One day you hear that Hannah's house will be raided next. You find Mahol.

"Please, will you help me warn a friend that Saul's men are on their way to her house? She's a widow near the old wall. Her name's Hannah," you say.

Mahol nods. "Sure. I like Hannah."

"You know Hannah?" You are surprised.

Mahol smiles. "She caught me stealing bread from her one day and has left out a slice for me every day since."

You smile. That sounds like Hannah. When Mahol leaves, you get to work. Saul and his men are headed for Hannah's house. You chase a flock of fowl into the street in front of them. The birds make a terrible racket with their squawking. Saul's men have to work their way around the birds. When they leave the fowl behind, you begin throwing pebbles at them from rooftops along their path. They stop to try to catch you, but you disappear into back alleys. You hear later that Hannah is safe.

Every day, you follow Saul's men and try to keep them from completing their job. One day as you are throwing pottery from the rooftops, a guard grabs you. He has been waiting for you there all day. He throws you into prison.

You do not care. You sing praises to God all day and night. You are surprised that your voice remains strong and loud. You have no desire to stop singing. They finally let you go because you have a terrible singing voice.

THE END

◆ ◆ ◆

You shrug. "Maybe they don't like my face." They laugh. You continue, "I fell into a flock of birds and got them all riled up."

The three of you hang out together, hiding in Joshua's home and eating leftover food for a few days. It begins tasting hard and stale, but you prefer any kind of food to going hungry. You enter and leave by a back window. You cannot help wondering what happened to your family. You want to search for them.

One day, you say, "I'm leaving Jerusalem. I want to start fresh somewhere else." You want to search for your family.

Beker looks upset. "You'll never find the pickings as good as they are here."

"Maybe," you say, "but I won't know until I've tried."

Mahol fingers a stale barley loaf. "I've been thinking of making some changes also."

Beker rolls her eyes. "Now I've heard everything."

"I'm serious," Mahol says. He looks at you. "I feel restless. It's time for a change. Maybe I'll go with you."

"Sounds good." You smile, but you do not feel like smiling. If Mahol goes with you, he will eventually figure out that you are a believer in Jesus. This could be dangerous for your family and you. It might even be dangerous for him.

CHOICE ONE: If you leave with Mahol the next day,
go to page 261.

CHOICE TWO: If you sneak away in the night and leave
Mahol behind, go to page 315.

◆ ◆ ◆

Y ou shrug. You cannot endanger your family by telling Mahol the truth.

"I've got my reasons," you say. "Can I count on you?"

"I've got nothing better to do," Mahol says.

"You're the best, Mahol," you say.

He shrugs. "By the way, you look awful, something like the shepherds I just saw in the marketplace. Of course, you don't smell as bad as they do. Are you okay?"

You nod.

"I'll make sure your family's safe," Mahol says. "Trust me." You cannot help feeling a little worried.

You punch him in the arm. "Okay, if you say so."

He takes off in one direction, and you go in another. What he said gave you an idea. You head for the market and find the shepherds. They look just as messy as you do. You watch them shopping for food and can tell they need help. The person they are about to buy from always doubles the prices for people from out of town.

You go up to the one who looks like the leader and quietly say, "Don't buy from that stand."

He looks at you and raises his eyebrows. You know he wonders if you are a thief trying to trick him to get his money. Who knows? Maybe you did steal from him before you became a follower of Jesus.

You smile. "I'm not a thief. You are not from here. I am, and I can show you where to buy better fruit at half the price."

"And what's in this for you?" he asks.

"I want to leave Jerusalem. If you will let me travel with you, I will feel safer."

He nods. "Not many people want to travel with shepherds. Where's the fruit?"

You lead them to the stands that have the best produce. When they leave Jerusalem, you go with them. No one ever notices shepherds, so the guards do not notice you. Your group joins other shepherds who stayed in the fields with the sheep. The flock is enormous.

You volunteer to help watch the sheep, and they give you a shift. After a few days, the leader says, "We are shorthanded. Would you like to stay with us?"

"I would," you say. It is nice to be around good people and to have friends. You send up a prayer for your family's safety.

That night around the fire, an older shepherd in the group tells a story. "On a night like this when I was young, a wonderful thing happened."

"And we haven't heard this story before," one man says, laughing.

"Shh!" says another. "The new kid hasn't heard it. Besides, I want to hear it again."

The old man continues, "I was watching sheep with some others near Bethlehem. Suddenly there was light all around us, and an angel appeared. I tell you, I was scared, so scared I thought my heart would stop beating. Trembling with fear, I was—"

"We know. You were afraid," the first man says. "Get on with the story."

"Anyway, the angel said, 'Don't be afraid.' That was easy for him to say. Then—I remember it like it was yesterday—he said, 'I bring you good news of great joy that will be for all the people. Today in the town of David a Savior has been born to you; He is Christ, the Lord.'"

The shepherd moves closer and looks straight at you.

"He was talking about the Messiah! Well, I tell you, I was shocked. Why would an angel come to us? And with such news! Can you believe it? He told us we'd find the baby in a feeding trough, a manger. I wondered why a mother would put her newborn in a place where cows and donkeys slobber. What if a cow got hungry in the night?"

"Go on, will you?" says the same shepherd. He stirs the fire, and red-hot ash rises in the air.

"Well, all at once, the whole sky was filled with angels, singing and praising God like nothing I'd ever heard before. Then just as fast, the sky was dark again. We all hurried to Bethlehem, and the baby was right where the angel said he'd be, all wrapped up in cloth. I think they cleaned the feed box out."

The youngest shepherd moves closer to the storyteller. His face shines in the light of the fire. "Tell us the best part."

"It was when that baby looked at me that I knew. He was our Savior, come straight to us from God. Well, we couldn't help ourselves. The whole way back to the fields, we praised the Lord for what we had seen. I left for another town soon after that. When I returned a few years later, I heard that King Herod had killed all the boys in Bethlehem ages two and under. I've always wondered . . ." His voice trails off.

Everyone is silent. You take a deep breath. "I know what happened to the baby. He grew up to be Jesus of Nazareth."

"The one the Romans killed?" one of the men asks.

You nod. "But he rose from the dead the third day afterward." You tell them everything you know about Jesus. "His death paid for all our sins. He made peace with God for us."

The old man's eyes light up. A slow smile crosses his face. He nods. "I believe." Then he stands up and throws out his arms. "Glory to God in the highest!"

THE END

Without a word to your family, you run to the window at the back of the house. You are afraid that you have put them all in danger. Maybe if the guards do not find you, they will leave your family alone. If they do arrest your family, you can help them escape, but only if you are free. You slide silently over the rough ledge of the window and blend into the darkness.

You whisper a quick prayer. "Help my family, please." You thank God that you got so much training about living on the streets. You climb to a nearby rooftop. You can see your family being taken away, even little Rachel. You follow them to see where they are taken. An urge deep inside of you wants to flee now, this very moment.

"I'm going to rescue my family first," you whisper to yourself. You are not sure where to turn, so you go to Hannah's house.

"I thought you might be back," she says. You are amazed that she does not reprimand you for the lateness of the hour or your messy appearance. She opens the door and then bars it behind you. She continues, "Are you hungry?"

You nod. She gives you part of the loaf that you brought to her earlier that day.

"You can sleep on that mat by the table," she says. "This can be your home until you have your family back."

How did she know? Your eyes are moist, and you feel yourself trembling. Hannah's arms feel warm and strong as she hugs you.

"Don't tell me where you go or what you do. Then they can't force or trick the information out of me."

You do not get much sleep. You roll onto your side, then your back, and then back to your side. All night you try to work out a plan to save your family.

CHOICE ONE: If you steal the keys to the prison door,
go to page 312.

CHOICE TWO: If you spend your time praying,
go to page 305.

◆ ◆ ◆

You give Eleazar another smile as you both enter through the gates of Jerusalem. "Yes, I'll join you." You wonder if he sees through your pretense. Does he suspect that you intend to warn families of the raids so they will be able to escape?

Eleazar nods. "Meet me here just after dark tonight."

"Who will we catch first?" you ask. You stumble over a rut in the street.

"Just be here," he says. His lips turn up. You nod, but his thin, sinister smile makes you nervous. You take a roundabout way home, making certain that no one is following you.

When you arrive home, you pull Joshua aside. "They've killed Stephen, and now they're going to raid the homes of all the believers. We'll all go to prison, or worse. I'm going to pretend to be one of them. That way I can try to warn our friends in time."

Joshua shakes his head, "Your intentions are worthy, but what you're doing is a lie. It will come to no good."

You shrug. "Perhaps you should leave Jerusalem. It would be safer."

"Where would we go?" he asks. "No, this is our home. My family has lived here for generations." Even the smell of the ground that formed these walls has a sense of home to it. You nod.

Yet, fear for these dear people that you have come to love grips your heart. You must help save them, somehow. That night, you meet Eleazar at the gate just after dark.

"Where are we headed?" you ask. Your teeth are chattering, but the weather is not even chilly.

"First, we meet Saul," he says.

"And then where?" you ask.

"Anywhere he tells us to go."

You follow Eleazar. Your legs feel wobbly, and your mouth has gone dry. You do not want other followers of Jesus to think that you have betrayed them, but you have to take this risk. You wonder if you will be brave enough to do whatever is required.

"There's Saul," Eleazar says. "They've already headed out." You follow behind them. At first, you do not realize what street you are on, until they stop outside of your house.

"No!" you scream. "Joshua! Anna! Get out! Run!" You continue screaming for your family to escape until you feel something heavy hit your head. You fall to the ground. A warm, sticky liquid drips into your eyes. You think it must be your own blood.

You lie in the street as the guards force their way into your house. You turn over to see if your family got away, but your head is spinning. You taste the dirt of the road, and you cannot lift your head.

Then you hear, "That foolish kid warned them. They've escaped!"

You smile to yourself and let the blackness overtake you.

THE END

◆ ◆ ◆

Y ou race to Simeon's house, running over rooftops to save time.
You jump down near his door and pound on it.

"Simeon," you gasp. "Simeon!"

Simeon opens the door. "What is it?"

"Soldiers are coming. They're coming to arrest you and your
family because you're believers. You've got to leave now. They're
almost here."

"Shomer! Maacah!" Simeon calls. Within seconds, his wife and
daughter are beside you in the street. You look over your shoulder. You can hear footsteps in the distance. Simeon whispers, "Take
them with you. I will remain to stall for time."

You do not argue. There is no time. You walk quickly down the
street with Shomer and Maacah. You are only houses away when
you hear pounding on Simeon's door. You force yourself not to look
back and continue at the same pace. Whatever happens, you must
not draw attention to yourselves.

"They are there," Maacah whispers. "They are at our house.
Father is still inside. What is going to happen to him?" Her voice
slowly begins to rise. "What is going to happen to us? How are we
going to survive? Will we ever see Father again?"

You say, "Shomer, go to the house on the center section of the old
wall by Elias's house. Do you know where I mean?" You see her nod,
and you continue, "Joshua and Anna are there. You can escape with
them if we get separated."

Maacah's voice begins to rise. "What will happen to Father?

You have to act fast. You push Maacah toward her mother.

CHOICE ONE: If you leave your friends and then direct the soldiers' attention somewhere else, go to page 270.

CHOICE TWO: If you put your hand over Maacah's mouth and continue at a slow pace, go to page 321.

From the road, you head north. As soon as you are out of sight of Jerusalem, you take off Anna's clothes and tie them into your tunic. You feel so much cooler.

You walk quickly. Your family could not be far ahead. They are pulling a heavy cart. You know, because you packed it well. By late afternoon, you catch up to them.

Naomi runs to you and holds you tightly. "I thought we would never see you again," she says. Joshua and Anna are next. Little Rachel is holding her arms up to you with her fingers wiggling back and forth.

"Carry me," she says.

You have been part of this family for such a short time, and yet they all love you. You thank God for them. Deep inside, you feel guilty about escaping through the window and leaving your family at the mercy of the guards. You place Rachel on the cart and pick up the handles to push.

"How about a ride?"

Rachel squeals in delight.

"I was going to hide the cart for you outside of Jerusalem. That's when I saw you leaving. I couldn't bring it to you because Saul's men were looking for me."

"How did you get out then?" Naomi asks.

You stop the cart. From within your tunic, you untie Anna's old clothes. You put them back on and hobble around the cart. Everyone laughs.

After several days, Joshua finds work as a carpenter in a small village in Judea. You also work hard to help your family, and whenever you get the chance, you tell people about Jesus.

THE END

"Mahol, Beker left to alert the authorities," you say.

Mahol nods. "Then I'd better talk faster." He continues preaching, and two others choose to follow Jesus. When the footsteps of officials draw close, all but the four of you flee.

The soldiers drag you to prison and throw you into a cell together. Then they take you out one by one. When it is your turn, your hands are tied to a metal loop. A guard takes his leather whip and flails it at your back.

"Ouch!" you cry involuntarily. The metal on the ends of the leather cuts into your back. The strokes continue. At the thirty-ninth lash, you feel as if you are going to pass out.

Then suddenly, they stop hitting you. They throw you back into your prison cell. It is cooler there and smells musty. The others have been beaten, too.

The pain is worse than any you have felt before, but you feel like laughing. Your friends join in. The joy of Jesus is everywhere. You teach the others a couple of songs. Every time you take a breath, the cuts on your back sting. Still, you want to praise God for saving Mahol and your two other friends. You all sing for about an hour.

The next morning, the soldiers release you with the warning, "Don't let us catch you telling others about Jesus!"

"I must obey God, no matter what you ask me to do," Mahol says. You prepare to be thrown back into prison, but they let you go anyway.

The four of you decide to leave Jerusalem. As you head out the gate together, Mahol says, "People all over the world need to hear about Jesus. Where should we start?"

You laugh. "Wherever the road leads, I guess."

With joy in your hearts, the four of you follow the road together.

THE END

You stay near Stephen and watch the other man drawing closer to you.

When he gets close enough to hear you, you say, "Good riddance."

The man raises his eyebrows. "What are you doing?"

You give a smile without humor. "I wanted to make sure this blasphemer was dead."

"I'm Eleazar," he says. You nod to him.

"I saw you with Saul earlier," you say. "I think that's his name. Is he in charge?" You walk out of the ditch toward Eleazar. You hope he cannot see how badly your legs are shaking.

"Saul is our leader," he said. "Thanks to him, things are going to change around here."

"How?" you ask. You both begin walking back toward Jerusalem. Part of you hates to leave Stephen's body alone, even though you know his spirit is with Jesus in paradise.

"We're going to raid the homes of blasphemers, these followers of Jesus," he says. "It's a false religion. We need to wash our country clean of them—in blood, if necessary."

"I see," you say. He is eyeing you suspiciously. You can feel yourself beginning to sweat.

"You can join us if you like," he says.

**CHOICE ONE: If you do not join Saul's men,
go to page 316.**

CHOICE TWO: If you join Saul's men, go to page 280.

"Help me!" you call to Beker and Mahol. The three of you quickly work together to climb up the side of a house. Within moments, you are running along the rooftops. Then without a word, you split up and run in different directions. You have done this routine so many times with your friends in the past. The sun's heat beats on your back. You jump down near the home of Simeon, a friend of Joshua's.

Keeping a careful eye, you work your way to Rabbi Levi's house and then dart into the alley behind it. A slight breeze goes by you. The fragrance of flowers is all around you. This is one of your old hangouts. It is not long before your other two friends meet you there.

Mahol says, "I hope what you stole was worth the trouble."

You hold out empty hands. "I didn't get anything for it."

"Oh," says Beker in disgust. "You mean we went through that and now have to hang low for nothing?"

Mahol says, "It's not like you to come back empty-handed. Why were those guards after you?"

CHOICE ONE: If you tell your friends that you are a follower of Jesus, go to page 299.

CHOICE TWO: If you shrug and change the subject, go to page 274.

"You'd better pack while I scout for an escape route," you tell your family.

Joshua agrees, "I do not know what we'd do without you." Joshua and Anna have meant so much to you. It makes you feel good that you are able to help them too. You give Joshua a hug before you leave the house.

Once on the street, you weave in and out of buildings and behind and over houses to find the right section of wall where your family can climb down. In an older area of town, you find a house on the wall of Jerusalem that you can easily climb. Even Rachel should be able to climb it with Anna's help. The way up this building is at the end of a narrow lane. It is dark and will keep you hidden from probing eyes.

"Now all I need is rope," you say to yourself. You go to the market and ask around.

"I'll give you some used rope," a merchant says, "in exchange for help unloading my carts." You inspect the used rope. It will work.

"I'll do it," you say. You think it is a good trade until you realize how many carts of vegetables he has. Sweat drips from your face. Splinters from the carts pierce your hands. It takes you hours to complete the task, but once it is done and you have the rope, you thank the man.

After carrying and lifting vegetables, your muscles are sore. The ropes feel heavy. You wrap them diagonally around your left shoulder and waist and hurry back to the building where your family will make their escape.

The ropes throw you off balance as you climb. The palms of your hands throb with the pain of blisters. About halfway up, you miss your footing. You touch only air. You hang by your fingers. The ropes grow heavier and heavier. They are weighing you down. You scramble with your feet for a ledge until you find one. Whew! That was close.

You continue climbing. You are almost to the roof—just one more reach with your arm. One rope starts slipping from its loop as someone comes out of the building. He walks directly below you. You hold tightly to the wall and try not to move so that you do not draw attention to yourself. When he is gone, you manage to swing yourself over the top edge of the roof.

Once you have checked the roof to make sure that it is safe, you look for a place to go down the outside wall. A large stone jutting from the inside top of the wall is perfect for tying the rope. You attach it and then cover the coil with hay stored on the roof. When your family arrives later, all you will have to do is let the rope down over the wall to the ground outside the city. You hide a second rope under the hay. Everything is set. You go home. The family is packed.

"We'll have to split up to avoid suspicion," you say.

Joshua nods. "We can meet after dark. Where should we meet?"

You explain to them where to go. Now all you have to do is wait. Anna and Naomi visit a friend. Joshua and Rachel stay at the house. You wait behind Rabbi Levi's house. Time passes slowly. Finally it begins growing dark. It is only moments now. You can feel your heart beating faster. Your hands are growing clammy. In the dimming light, you hear men talking behind a courtyard wall.

"When Benjamin gets here, we will go to Simeon the stonecutter's house. He's a follower of Jesus. We'll make an example of his family."

You know Simeon. He is a good man and a friend of Joshua. He is in great danger. If you warn Simeon, you could be putting your family in danger. If you do not warn Simeon, his family will be harmed. What should you do?

CHOICE ONE: If you warn Simeon, go to page 283.

CHOICE TWO: If you take care of your family,
go to page 257.

You fling the door open and try to fight the soldiers. You know that you are no match for their strength or their numbers.

"Run!" you scream. One hits your face with a stick. You ignore the pain. If only your family can escape, then the pain will be worth it. Another pushes you roughly from the doorway. You yell again, "Run! Run!"

The other soldiers push past you. You fall. They step on your hands and arms as they rush to grab Joshua, Anna, Naomi, and Rachel. Rachel starts to cry. You know she is afraid. A soldier knocks dishes to the ground. Another smashes the chair that Joshua made for Anna.

You sit up and try to fight harder, holding on to the legs of those around you. Again you are knocked to the floor before they drag you to prison. Once you are all in the prison cell, Anna examines your sores and bruises.

"You shouldn't have fought them," she says gently. Your cuts have stopped bleeding, but your body pulsates with pain.

"I must have led them to the house when I ran home to tell you about Stephen," you say. "I wasn't thinking. I'm sorry."

Joshua puts a hand on your shoulder. You wince but are glad to feel his strength. "We are glad you came home to tell us."

"Mommy, I'm scared," Rachel says. Anna opens her arms, and Rachel climbs into them.

Anna says, "Let's sing together." Her voice starts softly. Joshua joins her. Soon you are singing too. You know your days on earth may be numbered, but you feel God's peace as you sing. You would not want to be anywhere else than in His presence, which is where you are right now.

THE END

Y ou sneak back into your family's house. In the rag box, you find an old dress and veil that belonged to Anna. It is full of holes, but you wrap yourself in it, trying to look like a field worker. You leave your own clothes on underneath.

Then you search the house until you find a ragged-looking basket. You place it under your arm and walk toward the city gate. Maybe if you hobble a little, you will be more convincing. In fact, if you are bent over, you can hide your face! You try it.

"Old woman," the gatekeeper says as you draw near to the gate, "bring me some garlic when you return."

It worked! He must think you are going to work in the fields. You grunt as if in answer and then pass through the gate.

CHOICE ONE: If you head north to find your family, go to page 285.

CHOICE TWO: If you go into the fields and start working to avoid suspicion, go to page 314.

"That's great, Mahol," you say. "I wish I could go with you, but I have to find my family."

"I understand," Mahol says. "God has different work for each of us to do."

After spending a few more days together, you set off in opposite directions. You travel wherever the dusty road takes you, in search of your family. You survive on fish and the kindness of other believers in the areas where you travel. You look and look, all the time keeping Mahol and your family in your prayers. It is a solitary life, but you grow closer to God through it. Wherever you go, you tell people about Jesus. After ten years of searching, you find your family in a small village on the outskirts of Judea.

Anna recognizes you immediately. "You have come home!" Soon Joshua wraps his strong arms around you. You did not realize how much you had missed them. You cry tears of joy. Soon Rachel and Naomi are hugging you, too. They have grown much taller.

You settle down in their village and become a basket weaver and storyteller. The village children gather around every day to hear the stories of your travels and how God used you to bring people to Jesus. Life is very, very good.

THE END

"Those guards were about to arrest my adopted father," you say. "Joshua did something wrong?" Beker asks. You are surprised that she knows his name.

You shake your head no. "He is a follower of Jesus."

Mahol nods, knowingly. "Saul asked the Council for permission to hunt down Jesus' followers."

"We were going to leave Jerusalem," you say, "but they recognized Joshua. I had to think of something fast so he could get through the gate."

Beker takes a step away from you and acts like she's studying the rough stones in the wall. "So you're a follower, too?"

"Yes."

"I'm getting out of here," she says, and darts away.

Mahol hesitates, looking like he might leave, too. Then he turns around and sits on the ground beside you. "I'd like to ask you some questions. What makes this Jesus fellow so important? Why is the town so divided on who this one man is?"

"Because He isn't just a man. He's God," you say.

Mahol wants to understand. You talk together late into the night. Finally he says, "I want to follow Jesus too."

You smile. "Then tell Jesus you're sorry for your sins and that you believe He is God."

"In case you haven't noticed, Jesus isn't here," he says.

"You tell him from your heart," you say. You both hear footsteps.

"I will," he promises. His face looks concerned, and he immediately scrambles up the wall next to you.

Suddenly guards grab your hands. You are so surprised that you do not fight back.

They throw you into prison. The floor is hard and feels cold. You shiver most of the night and catch a cold. After a few days, your cold worsens. You begin to cough a lot. Then one day, you are allowed a visitor. Mahol walks in with a smile.

Even before he whispers, "I'm a follower of Jesus now," you can tell he is because of the joy in his eyes. He continues, "I'll find a way to get you out of here."

You shake your head no. "Find my family," you say. "Tell them that I'm okay."

"But I can't leave you here," he says. "I have a plan to help you escape."

"No," you say. "I want to stay here. If I escape, that soldier over there would be killed. He's responsible. I've been telling him about Jesus. He doesn't like hearing it, but maybe he'll listen after a while. I've been praying for him."

Mahol looks at you strangely. "I've never met anyone like you."

"It's only Jesus who makes me act like this," you say. "Please go to my family."

Mahol nods. "All right, but I'll see you again."

You nod. "If not on earth, then in heaven."

As he leaves, it almost looks like there is a tear sliding down his face. You give him a smile. You are glad that he is gone, because you can feel your cough coming back. You cough deeply and cannot seem to stop. It hurts to breathe. You know you are dying.

The soldier gives you a drink of water. It is the first kindness he has shown you. Each day, you get worse and worse, but you still pray for the soldier and tell him how much God loves him. You thank him for taking care of you.

Then one day, the soldier says, "Why do you care so much about me? I've done little for you."

"Because Jesus lives in me, and He loves you more than you can imagine."

The soldier listens while you explain how Jesus can save him from his sins and give him eternal life with God. Just before you die, you have the joy of knowing that the soldier has become a brother in Christ.

THE END

◆ ◆ ◆

Although you want to scream, you hold it in. You try to blend into the crowd. It seems like forever until the angry men around you leave for the city. From what they say, you can tell they think they just did something pleasing to God. You know that the penalty for blasphemy is death by stoning, but Stephen would never dishonor God or His name.

You do not want to draw suspicion to yourself, so you start toward the city with the others. When no one is looking, you circle back around and hurry to Stephen's side. You hope he is alive.

You struggle to lift the heavy stones off his body. He does not seem to be breathing.

"Stephen, I'm here," you say. "Wake up."

He does not move. "Are you dead? Please don't be dead."

Just then you look up. In the distance, a man is watching you. He was one of the men with Saul. You try to find any sign of life in Stephen. His body is still warm, but he is dead. You stand up.

CHOICE ONE: If you trick Saul's follower into believing you are one of them, go to page 289.

CHOICE TWO: If you go back into Jerusalem, go to page 303.

◆ ◆ ◆

You look away from the man and hurry back to Jerusalem by another route. Once inside the city, you know that you cannot return to your family's home. That would put them into too much danger.

With a sigh, you go back to living on the streets. You plan to leave Jerusalem, but you want to warn your family first. You hang out near the Temple and meet up with Mahol.

"Where have you been, stranger?" he says. Mahol knows how to find information. You tell him about your new home with Joshua and Anna.

"I've seen you with them," he says.

You point to the Council chamber. "What's going on inside?"

"The Council just gave Saul the power to put people into prison."

"Who? What people?" you ask. You hope you sound casual enough not to make him suspicious. You lean against the smooth wall surrounding the chamber.

"The followers of Jesus. Weren't you one of them? Hey, maybe there's a reward out for you."

You laugh. "There's no reward. Who would want me?"

Mahol laughs. "Just asking."

"I would like to get a message to the family I was with," you say. "I want them to know that I'm safe. But living with them . . . well . . . they need to know I'm not coming home. And if what you say is true, they need to leave town."

"They were good to you, weren't they?" Mahol asks.

"They were great," you say.

"Why don't you want to go back?"

"It's a long story." You stare at the Temple steps.

CHOICE ONE: If you do not tell him the true reason,
go to page 275.

CHOICE TWO: If you tell him the truth, go to page 263.

You go back to your family's house and pray. Saul's men may be watching the house, so you stay out of sight. You ignore your growling stomach and spend all your time praying to God for the release of your family.

Finally, you clean yourself up, straighten the house, and pack everything that is of value. You find an old cart in back and load all of your family's belongings onto the cart. You plan to hide the cart in the hills outside of Jerusalem. Everything will be waiting for them whenever they get out of prison.

You leave and walk boldly down the street with the cart. You are strong enough to easily hold the handles and keep everything in its place. You know that God is with you. You see others looking at you strangely; you are drawing too much attention. You park the cart in an alleyway and hide. From the coolness of the shadows you watch.

You notice guards are escorting some people through the gates, forcing them to leave the city. You are overjoyed to see that Joshua, Anna, Rachel, and Naomi are among them. You breathe deeply. God has been so good to you.

You see Beker behind you and wave to her. "Over here."

She joins you. "Long time no see."

You nod. "I need your help." When you explain, she rolls her eyes, but takes the cart out of the city to Joshua.

When Beker returns, she tells you, "I don't think your family was expecting their things. They seemed pretty surprised." She backs up as if she is going to leave.

"Thank you," you say. You give her a wide smile. "You've done a very good thing today."

She shrugs. "They seemed happy to hear that you were safe." She stops as if a fight is going on inside of her. "Oh, here." She plops something into your hand. It is Anna's gold ring. "They wanted you to use this for money until you can get to them." She turns to leave, but you grab her hand and put the ring back into it.

"God gives me everything I need," you say. "Take this in payment for what you did for me and my family." You see a moment of uncertainty in Beker's face before she smiles and closes her fist over the ring.

"Your loss," she says and disappears into the crowd.

Your prayers have been answered. Your family has escaped. Unfortunately, Saul's men are still looking for you.

CHOICE ONE: If you sneak out of Jerusalem in a merchant's cart, go to page 259.

CHOICE TWO: If you dress like a field worker and try to go through the gate, go to page 297.

You take a deep breath. It would feel so good to try to get back at Saul and his followers for what they did to your family. Just then you remember Stephen's words: "Do not hold this sin against them." You try to concentrate on your family and not on your anger.

As soon as you arrive back at the house, you begin packing your few belongings.

Joshua smiles. "I'm glad you will be with us."

"Where will we go? What will we do?" you ask.

"Wherever God tells us to go and whatever God tells us to do."

You had forgotten that God is still in charge. You help Naomi tie her belongings into a blanket. Many things must be left behind. You take only what you can carry. With one last look at the only home you have ever known, you head for the nearest gate with your family. For a moment, it is a little tense. The gatekeepers are checking everyone. You see them eyeing Anna's face. Her veil does not quite hide the cuts and bruises.

"It isn't going to work," you say under your breath to Joshua.

Joshua puts his hand on your arm. "Sometimes when things seem their worst, God is doing His finest." You are behind a cart of garlic. One step. Two steps. After the cart owner is a man on a horse, and then your family is next. You try not to look at the guards.

"Hey you," says one of the soldiers. He is pointing at Joshua.

Just then, the cart of garlic stops abruptly. The horse bumps into the cart. It tips. Garlic spills everywhere. In the confusion, you and your family walk through the gate without being stopped. You turn back to see what caused the commotion. The donkey pulling the cart had sat down and was refusing to move.

You want to laugh and yell and dance, but you follow Joshua at a slow pace. As much as you try to stop it, a grin breaks out on your face.

Joshua looks at you and his eyes twinkle. "It isn't the first time that God used a donkey to deliver His people."

The air is fresh. The sun is warm. It does not matter where you are headed. The Lord will guide you. You are overjoyed to be alive and with your very own family.

THE END

"I'll go with you," you say. You want to find your family, but there is little chance of meeting up with them again. Mahol has helped you see how important it is to tell others about Jesus. You would never have believed that Mahol would become a follower. Perhaps more of your friends would believe if you could find the courage to tell them. You pray for that courage.

You both join a caravan that is heading toward Jerusalem. One by one, each member of the caravan hears about God's Son, Jesus, from Mahol. Although no one chooses to believe, they seem to like Mahol. Once you have reached the outskirts of Jerusalem, the leader draws you and Mahol aside and gives you both a sweet, gritty fig to chew on while he talks.

"Do not be so loud in your praise of Jesus once you are in Jerusalem. I wish you to live long lives."

Mahol gives him a grin. "Thank you for your concern, but with Jesus, we have eternal life already. Remember, you can have it too."

Once inside, you go in search of your old friends. Beker and five others are hanging out in an alley.

"Guess what!" Mahol says. "I have to tell you about something exciting. I have met God through His Son, Jesus Christ."

Because everyone respects Mahol, they listen. After a while, you see Beker slowly moving away from the group. In the pit of your stomach, you feel that she is going to tell the officials that Mahol is a follower of Jesus.

CHOICE ONE: If you tell Mahol what Beker is doing, go to page 287.

CHOICE TWO: If you follow Beker, go to page 318.

Although it is late afternoon by the time you all have your belongings packed, the gate is still open. As a family, you decide to leave immediately. After Stephen's stoning, the thieves in the surrounding hills seem less scary than the religious leaders inside Jerusalem.

You separate from one another so you will not draw attention to yourselves. First Anna and Rachel leave through the gate together. No one questions what they are doing. You breathe a sigh of relief. Then Naomi walks through. She has all her belongings in a basket on her head. Although it is the wrong time for girls to go out to the fields, you hope the guards will think she is a worker. She passes through the gates without drawing attention to herself.

Casually leaning against a stall in the market, you wait. Joshua begins his walk through the marketplace and toward the gate. Just then you see two men pointing to Joshua. They are talking together and nodding their heads.

CHOICE ONE: If you signal Joshua with a whistle to tell him there is trouble, go to page 317.

CHOICE TWO: If you create a diversion, go to page 266.

◆ ◆ ◆

Y ou want to protect your friends, so you go back down the alley to try to escape. A soldier is waiting for you at the end.

"No one steals while I'm on watch," he says. He holds you in a viselike grip. It is impossible to get away from him. He throws you into prison. It is dirty. It is dank. It is dark.

For some odd reason, though, you are not depressed. You feel God's peace inside of you. As you sit there in the dark, you praise God and pray for your family and all the believers in Jerusalem.

Then, just as you are getting sleepy, you see a bright light. You hear praises to God, even though the cell remains quiet. An angel appears at your cell door. A sweet fragrance like spring flowers surrounds you. The angel motions for you to follow him. You think you must be dreaming. You follow the angel out of prison and to the gates of Jerusalem. The angel opens the gates and then shuts them softly behind you. When the gates shut, the sounds, smells, and light disappear.

You rub your eyes. You have escaped! Nothing is impossible for God!

You do not know where you are headed or if you will find your family, but that does not worry you. God is in charge. Wherever you go and whatever you do, He will provide.

THE END

In the morning, you leave early so no one will see that you were at Hannah's house. You do not want her to get into trouble too. You find an alley across from the prison where you can watch the guards coming and going. Pressing your body against the rough walls, you hide in the shadows. You notice who has the prison keys and who does not.

That night, you stay in the alley. You sleep on the dusty ground and watch the soldiers whenever you are not sleeping. In the middle of the night, you see your opportunity. One of the prison guards is sitting so that his right side is facing the alley across from you. You weave around back streets and between buildings to get to that alley. As silently as you can, you creep close to him. The prison keys are attached to a leather rope on his belt.

Who would have thought that your training as a thief would come in so handy? You have never stolen anything from a guard before now. Slowly you ease up behind him. You are within inches. His back leans against the building, and his arms are crossed over his chest.

If you can just untie the leather band, then the keys will be yours. Slowly you work the leather so that the soldier cannot feel your tugs. Just as you are about to get the key ring, there is a noise to the soldier's left.

He stands up quickly. As he does so, the key ring falls to the ground. The sound seems enormous to your ears. You think about grabbing the keys and running, but you know you would be caught. You melt into the alley's shadows. The soldier picks up the ring and reties it. You retrace your steps back to your place on the other side of the street.

For two days you watch for another opportunity, but none appears. Finally one day you see your new family being released from prison. When they are a few blocks from the prison, you join them. As you draw closer, you can tell that Anna and Joshua have been beaten. They are glad to see you.

"We didn't know what happened to you. How did you get away?"

"Through the window. I've been trying for days to find a way to rescue you."

"They warned us never to talk about Jesus again," Anna says.

"Are you going to obey them?" you ask.

"No!" little Rachel says. Everyone laughs, but you can feel anger welling up inside of you. This is your family. They are good people. They should not have been treated so badly just because they believe in Jesus.

Joshua tells you that they must leave Jerusalem. "Will you be coming with us?"

CHOICE ONE: If you leave Jerusalem with your family, go to page 307.

CHOICE TWO: If you stay in Jerusalem to try to sabotage the men who are persecuting followers of Jesus, go to page 272.

◆ ◆ ◆

You go into the fields and start working. You tear out what you think are weeds.

A woman shouts, "Why are you pulling up the barley? Do you want to starve us all? Get out of here!"

How could you know? You have never worked in the fields before. Until a few months ago, you were just a street kid. Anna's clothes start slipping off. A girl not far from you starts laughing and pointing. You throw off Anna's bulky clothes and run for the hills. Everyone is laughing. No one follows.

You hide out in the hills for a few days. You eat figs from a tree and drink water from a neighboring farmer's well. You do not know where your family went, but you believe that God will keep them safe. In the morning, you find a road and follow it. Whatever direction it takes you, you are determined to serve the Lord as long as you live.

THE END

When you are sure that both Beker and Mahol are asleep, you sneak out of the house through the back window. You dart in and out of shadows through the streets of Jerusalem until you find a place in the wall to climb down the other side.

Once free, you realize that you have nowhere to go. You have concentrated so hard on escaping that you never even considered what you would do once you left. You decide that Samaria is as safe a place as any. Perhaps you will discover news of your family there.

You find a cave in the hills where you can sleep that night. Tomorrow, you will take the first step into your new life.

THE END

◆ ◆ ◆

You know that if you do not offer to help Saul, this man will suspect you are a follower of Jesus. Still, you look down and shake your head.

"No," you say. "I'm not ready for that."

He shrugs. "To each his own."

When he leaves, you turn around and go back outside the city. You cannot put your family at risk by going home. You walk for a while, not knowing what to do. The path is hard and dusty. As you walk, a plan forms in your head. You can live off the land and keep an eye on the road. If your family leaves the city, you will be able to spot them. You think you know which road they will use.

You find a place that is high enough for you to see the road, but low enough so that others will not find you. Waiting is difficult. You have always preferred action. Now all you can do is pray. On second thought, that is the best thing you can do. When you are not hunting for food, you spend your time praying for your family and the other believers in Jerusalem.

Weeks go by, and then one day, you see them. You wait for your family to get a safe distance from the gate before you run down the hill toward them.

"Joshua! Anna!" you shout.

They are surprised to see you. When Anna and the girls finally stop hugging you, Anna says, "We thought you had been killed. Where have you been?"

You tell them about what happened after Stephen was stoned. "I was afraid they would hurt you because of me." They hug you again and again. As a family, you leave for another area far away from Jerusalem.

THE END

◆ ◆ ◆

You signal Joshua to tell him he is in trouble, but it is too late. The two men move forward. Two guards are with them. Everything happens at the same time. The guards grab Joshua's arms. Joshua sees you running forward to help. Your eyes meet.

In a loud voice, he says, "Do as you like to me. God gave me a brave child to take care of my family when I am gone!"

You stop. Joshua said those words not to the guards but as a message for you. He wants you to leave and help Anna and your sisters escape. Your heart aches. You hear Joshua struggling with the soldiers. You want to save him, but what can you do? Although you feel a horrible pain in your heart, you obey Joshua. His arrest has created the confusion you need to walk through the gates without being stopped.

"They got Joshua," you tell Anna. "He told me to take care of you."

You can see the tears in her eyes, but she nods and takes the hands of each of her girls.

"We'll wait for him in Samaria," you say, but you have little hope of seeing him. Once again Anna nods, as if she cannot trust her voice.

In Samaria, you find work as a shepherd and take care of your family all your days. You never see Joshua again. When you remember him, you thank God for giving you a father, even for such a short time. Joshua showed you God's love firsthand. Throughout your life, you try to follow Joshua's example and show that same love to others.

THE END

◆ ◆ ◆

You trail Beker so that she does not know you are following her. From the direction she is heading, you can tell that she is going directly to the Council. You wonder if she has been one of their spies all along. She would be able to tell them where the followers of Jesus lived. She is smart enough. Just before she goes into the building, you dive for her, and the two of you wrestle on the street.

When she stops struggling, you hold her down and ask her, "What are you doing?"

Her lips tighten. She does not say a word.

"You can turn me in, if you like," you say, "but leave Mahol and the others out of it." Beker turns her head away from you. You continue, "You know . . . Jesus died for you, too."

"More lies," she says.

"The truth," you say. You have gotten dirt in your mouth, but there is nowhere for you to spit it out.

Beker struggles again, but you do not release your hold. "You don't care about your friends," she says. "You went and lived with Joshua and Anna. Then you took Mahol away. You both deserted me."

You never realized how alone Beker must have felt.

"I'm sorry. I should have included you. Beker, Jesus really does love you. He died so that you can be forgiven for all your sins." You let go of her and sit on the ground beside her. She sits up.

"I don't believe it. He can't forgive me. I've done too many bad things."

You put your arm around her shoulders. "We've all done too many bad things. That's why Jesus had to come. He would have come even if you were the only one who needed Him. That's how much He loves you."

She looks away. You are not sure why until you hear her sniffle. She is trying to hide her tears. You have never seen this softer side of Beker.

You give her time to get control of her emotions before you say, "Beker, let's go back to Mahol."

She nods. You walk back together in silence. Seven days later when you leave Jerusalem, five of you leave as followers of Jesus. Beker is one of the five.

You travel together to Samaria, and you find your family already living there.

"You are good children," Anna says. "Joshua, can't we do something for each of them?"

"I don't know," Joshua says. "But I was talking with Gideon the other day. He's a brick maker. He was looking for a young man who would want to learn his trade."

Mahol's eyes light up.

Joshua smiles. "Mahol, would you be interested?"

"Oh, yes," he says.

"And I know someone who has always wished for a daughter," Anna says. "Would you be interested, Beker?"

"A family? A family of my own? Oh, please, yes!" She hesitates. "Would you please introduce me as Rebecca?" Everyone laughs.

"Of course."

By the end of the year, each one of the former street kids has found a trade or a family in the community.

THE END

◆   ◆   ◆

You tell your boss you will be leaving with Palti, who has now become your friend. He sends someone else to watch the sheep. Originally, you thought that Palti was fleeing Jerusalem because he was scared, but after traveling with him for a few days, you realize that he is not afraid.

Warming his hands by the fire one night he says, "God has called me to go beyond Judea and preach the name of Jesus there."

"Do you mean that you left Jerusalem so you can go tell others about Jesus?"

He nods.

"But what if they beat you or even kill you for what you say?" you ask. You do not tell him that you fled Jerusalem as a coward. What would he say if he knew that you were afraid of the Jewish leaders? You draw circles in the dirt.

Palti shrugs. "I've already been beaten and imprisoned. The worst they can do is kill my body. They can't take away my faith or God's Holy Spirit that lives inside me."

What he says makes sense. Although you do not want to go through the pain of persecution, you know that your life is in God's hands. Even if you die, He will take you to live with Him forever.

"I'd like to learn to tell others about Jesus," you say.

Palti smiles. "You have plenty of time to learn. We're in for an amazing adventure."

THE END

Y ou cover Maacah's mouth as you continue walking. Her spit gets
on your hand, but you do not move your fingers.

Shomer grabs her daughter's arm. "Maacah, stop it. What if your
father escapes only to find that we have been killed because you
started to scream?"

Maacah's eyes suddenly clear. She relaxes. You pull your hand
away and wipe it on your robe. You have not broken your stride.

Her mother continues. "God is with us even in our trouble.
Trust Him."

Shomer's words seem to calm Maacah even more. They help
you, too.

You turn down one street and then another, looking behind you
at every turn. When you are certain that you have not been followed,
you go to the housetop where you hope your family is waiting. You
are extremely late. You help Maacah and Shomer climb to the roof.

Joshua is waiting for you. Joshua has already let down Anna and
the girls. You greet each other warmly but silently. You can see a
question in his eyes when he sees Shomer and Maacah. He looks for
Simeon, but you shake your head.

He ties another rope securely, and you work together to help
Shomer and Maacah down. Then you and Joshua climb down
together. You hide the ropes the best you can. Perhaps others will
need them after you.

Once you are away from the walls, you explain, "Saul's men were
after Simeon's family. I had to do something."

"I'm proud of you," Joshua says. "Thank you for helping our

friends." It makes you feel warm inside that he trusts you and your decisions. He continues. "We will take Shomer and Maacah to Bethlehem. Then we will see where God leads us."

You nod. You do not care where you go, as long as you are with those you love.

THE END

Go Deeper!

QUESTIONS AND IDEAS

DEADLY EXPEDITION

THINK ABOUT IT:

The Israelites were God's people. As often as they turned their back on him, He saved them. God was sad and angry that His people wandered from Him, but He continued to give them opportunities to turn back to Him. Think about the times God forgave you and welcomed you back even after you had made poor choices. Praise Him for His grace and love.

TALK ABOUT IT:

Telling others that you have committed your life to God not only cements your faith, but it also encourages others to grow in theirs. Ask your pastor or youth leader if you may give a testimony in church or Sunday school. The leader might want to hear what you plan to say and to help you come up with the right words.

TRY IT:

Sometimes God reveals His will in a very personal way. Sometimes He allows us to live within His general plan. Read the Bible and pray every day, alone and with others, to better understand God's plan for your life. Sometimes obeying God is difficult, but obedience always results in greater faith and a better life.

TRAPPED!

THINK ABOUT IT:

We do not worship gods of stone and wood, but we sometimes put things before our worship of God: money, friends, self. Ask God to help you think about what you value more than God. Ask God to forgive you for having another "god." Also ask Him to fill you with His Spirit so that you can honor only Him.

TALK ABOUT IT:

Be bold about your faith in the one true God. Make decisions based on who you are in Christ and then talk about it with others. This will increase your faith, build up others, and honor God. When you struggle with your faith, talk about that, too. God blesses the person of integrity.

TRY IT:

Don't just ask God for things. Spend time worshiping Him. Tell Him what you love about Him. Thank Him. God is so good: There is no darkness in Him at all! Once you get started in praising Him for that, you won't want to quit.

ATTACK!

THINK ABOUT IT:

What do you want to do with your life? Do you have grand plans and great goals? God planted those passions in your heart, and He gave you the ability to do it. On the other hand, if you're not quite sure what you will do when you grow up, that's okay. It's great to be open to different ideas that God might give you. Either way, make sure to spend time in prayer, asking the Holy Spirit to direct your steps.

TALK ABOUT IT:

Sometimes it is hard to obey. Some of the things God or parents or teachers or even presidents ask us to do are really hard. Lots of Christians struggle with this issue. Find a pastor or a parent or Christian friend to talk to about how you feel. God wants us to be real with Him. Only then will you be able to obey Him with joy.

TRY IT:

If you want God to trust you with the big stuff, you have to be able to handle the little stuff. That means: Obey your parents, do the nitty-gritty of homework and chores well and with a good attitude, be kind even to your little brother or sister, listen to good advice—those kinds of things. God will reward you. And you will be much happier.

ESCAPE!

THINK ABOUT IT:

Have you ever told a friend to watch a movie that you hated? Have you ever talked for hours about a book you couldn't stand? Of course not! If you want to endorse something, you have to believe in it. The same thing goes with sharing your faith. Spend time in prayer and Scripture every day, praying that the Holy Spirit will reveal Himself to you so you will become a person of great faith.

TALK ABOUT IT:

When you are excited about something, you naturally want to tell people about it. As you grow more in love with God, you will see all kinds of exciting things happen. When you tell your friends about what God has done for you, you don't have to try to convince them to become a Christian; you just have to tell them what you know. The Holy Spirit will do the rest.

TRY IT:

Some people think *integrity* is good behavior. It is actually living out what you believe. So, if you are a person of integrity and you say that you love Jesus, you will try to walk in step with the Spirit. If you want your friends to know that your faith is for real, you have to do what you know is right, avoid what you know is wrong, and say you're sorry when you mess up. Not only will your friends trust you more, but also you will be a happier person.

ABOUT THE AUTHORS

Jeanne Gowen Dennis is the host of Heritage of Truth TV, an award-winning author and songwriter, and a Colson Center Fellow and Centurion. She loves reading and spending time with children, especially her three amazing grandchildren.

Sheila Seifert is the director of parenting content for *Thriving Family* magazine, a marriage and parenting publication published by Focus on the Family. She has cowritten over 20 books, has had over 1,000 freelance sales, and has had a script air on PBS. She is the founder of Simple Literature and has taught writing, literature, and reading at the university level.